Price Road
Let's Talk About It

a Novel

by Elaine T. Jones

To McKinley
Thanks for your
support

Elaine T. Jones

iUniverse, Inc.
New York   Bloomington

Price Road

Let's Talk About It

Certain characters in this work are historical figures, and certain events portrayed did take place. However, this is a work of fiction. All of the other characters, names, and events as well as all places, incidents, organizations, and dialogue in this novel are either the products of the author's imagination or are used fictitiously.

iUniverse books may be ordered through booksellers or by contacting:

iUniverse
1663 Liberty Drive
Bloomington, IN 47403
www.iuniverse.com
1-800-Authors (1-800-288-4677)

ISBN: 978-0-595-48366-2 (pbk)
ISBN: 978-0-595-60457-9 (ebk)

Printed in the United States of America

iUniverse rev. date: 2/11/2009

This novel by E.T. Jones is a delightful detailed tale about people living in a segregated region where relationships are developed through the eyes of a postman. Through her characters, she tells of the struggles and trials that happened due to segregation in this economically strife-ridden region. Further, through the author's religious undertones, she shows how integration should evolve to work. Although fictional, Price Road is a clever book whose characters spring to life.

- Dr. Lois S. Miller

This is a book that was thoroughly researched by its author. The characters are many but interesting; a truly enlightening chronicle about the southern way of life.

- Midge Jackson

Every so often a book will come along that makes you truly glad that you got to read it; one that is so well written that it has the ability to take the reader to another place and time. A book that spans every human emotion and speaks to all people regardless of their station in life, yet one that tells such a beautiful story that you never want it to end. Amazingly complex in its content, yet beautifully simplistic in its style - I believe that Price Road is just such a book.

- Gene Barbero

Contact the author – etjstories@yahoo.com

To the Creator, and his love of variety.

To those who respect the diversity in their world,
and are not afraid to talk about it.

To my parents and grandparents who were dream carriers.

To my children: Dana, Kia, Chanda, and Becky, and my grandchildren
to whom I will pass the dream carrier's torch.

To Gwen Daniels, my best sister/ friend.

To Michelle Bush and Darlene Christie for help that earned them angel wings.

ROUTE #1

Price Road, otherwise known as Route #1, was one of the several rural highways that entwined into the small cluster of residential and business structures known as Leaksville, a small town in North Carolina. Located on intrastate highway #700, not far from the borderline where the vast green farmlands of North Carolina blended into the industrial mill town of Danville, VA., Leaksville was rather easy going and ethereal. Its extremities brushed the north side of the coveted shoreline of the famous Dan River where it joined the Smith River. The town was named for John Leak, who received about one hundred acres of land from Robert Galloway, a prominent land owner. God put forth his best efforts in the creation of this part of North Carolina; it was a picturesque area with a scenic landscape and fertile earth. The territory that comprised all of Spray, Draper, and Leaksville (small cities that composed the Tri-city area), was appropriately known as "The Wonderful Land of Eden."

There were only a few dreadfully poor White families sprinkled throughout the rural landscape along Price Road. The majority of White people in the tri-city area lived within the city limits; they had nice homes, good jobs, successful businesses, and went to work in suits. The five original streets laid out in Leaksville were Washington and Jay streets - which ran east and west, and Patrick, Henry, and Hamilton streets - which ran north and south. There were only a few Negro families that actually lived within the city limits of Leaksville, and almost all of them lived on or in close proximity to Henry Street - the one street that was the hub of the neighborhood for the Colored townsfolk. The colored store, Elks Home, church, funeral home, doctor's office, and residential homes were all pent-up within a three block strip of Henry Street. There was no hospital in Leaksville for the Negro population; however, there was a ward in the basement of the Morehead hospital for the colored patients who desperately needed care. Most of the sick in the colored community were treated in their own homes by doctors who did home visits; the babies were born at home and tended by a midwife.

Price Road rolled through the rural extension that began at the Leaksville city limit sign; therefore, the people who lived on Price Road were automatically categorized as country folk. Some houses, on this country landscape, were so far back from the highway that they couldn't be seen by a traveler along the road. Every rural household was represented by a mailbox at the roadside. All the metal tube-shaped mailboxes were secured atop a sturdy wood 2" x 4" support about the height of a six year old child.

Each family was responsible for posting the prevailing family name on the side of their mail box. Some names were hard to read because of meager printing skills, or they were faded from weather and age; regardless, the mailman, Ed O'Reilly, always knew which mail went where. Ed knew all of the families on his route, personally, because he had worked as their mail carrier for over fourteen years.

As he drove down Price Road, on his last official run on his mail route, Ed found it was hard for him to merge his conflicting emotions because he felt both sad and exhilarated. He had received a job promotion, and after a much needed two week vacation, Ed planned to start his new position as a supervisor at the Leaksville post office. The job change filled Ed with both sorrow and excitement because it provided a better income for his family, yet it took him away from his many friends on Price Road.

Ed graduated from Leaksville High School in June of 1940, two months before his eighteenth birthday. He served in the United States Army during 1941 and 1942; then, Ed returned home without injury, in 1943, as a World War II veteran. In September of that year he married Suellen, his high school sweetheart.

Ed's Uncle, Matthew O'Reilly, who was the Leaksville postmaster at that time, hired Ed to deliver mail for the United States Postal Service to the mostly colored community on Price Road (Route #1 as it is known for postal addresses). It was difficult for anyone who was the postmaster to keep a steady mail carrier for Route #1 because most White folks did not want to work at any job that might be construed as a service to the colored population. In 1943 a mail carrier, a government position, was not one of the job options for Colored people. It was 1954 before employment segregation ended in the U.S. Government, including the military, when President Eisenhower issued an executive order for desegregation. Therefore, in 1943, Ed's uncle, postmaster Matthew O'Reilly was relieved of a consistent employment issue when Ed agreed to accept the position. Ed was the only person Matthew knew who would take the job - who did not mind working on Price Road.

Price Road was one of several roads that joined the rural residents of Rockingham County North Carolina to the neighboring small towns. For example, Route #17 connected the towns of Leaksville and Reidsville as Route#1[Price Road] connected the towns of Leaksville and Stoneville. Price Road extended between Stoneville and Leaksville as a long, two lane, tarred highway; it rambled over about twenty country miles. The residents along Price Road always detected a substitute driver according to the time of the mail delivery, a substitute was usually late; Ed O'Reilly always arrived at the same time everyday.

After fourteen years, Ed O'Reilly still looked forward to the start of each day. He loved his job, and the people along his route respected him because of his proficiency and strong work ethics. He approached his assignment on Route #1 as a labor of love, and carried out his duties with organized efficiency. The mail car was easy to identify from a distance because Ed drove dreadfully slow; the car clung to the right side of the road, and made a loud knocking sound like a tin can with one lone rock being tossed around inside.

The old folks said, "*If a job is worth doing, it is worth doing well. Do it well or not at all*"

Ed always spent a few minutes parked beside each cluster of mailboxes. He envisioned the mailboxes as a monotone row of metal flowers planted in the dirt, parallel to the paved Price Road. Ed could tell whenever there was outgoing mail for him to pick up because an attached swing arm, shaped like a flag, was placed in the upright position on the mailbox. Over the years some of those mail notification flags were worn off; therefore, the mailbox owners, who were aware of how much Ed enjoyed beautiful flowers, showed their creativity by leaving a flower or two as an alternative signal. Dandelions, daffodils, or an assortment of wild flowers picked from the side of the road were placed through the clasp on the front of the mailbox as if they were in a flower vase.

Ed developed his own delivery routine. He deliberately stretched his left arm across the passenger seat of his unmarked seven year old faded gray Ford mail-car where the mailbag was stored. He bent deeply as he reached out of the open car window, on the passenger side, to attend to each mailbox. Ed was always careful to make sure his left foot exerted the necessary extra pressure on the brakes while the car was at a momentary standstill. Some days he accumulated enough of the 'signal flowers' to fashion a beautiful bouquet to take home to his wife; it made Suellen feel loved and contributed to keeping his home happy. Ed woke up every morning with fresh enthusiasm, he knew he was a fortunate man; he had good health, a good job, and beautiful flowers to fill the day. Who could ask for more? Although Ed was happy about his promotion, he was going to miss the daily routine he had grown to enjoy. Nevertheless, Ed felt a measure of satisfaction; his replacement, Leaksville's first Black mail-carrier, was a man he had recommended for the position. Ed hoped that was an indication that the field of job opportunity was leveling.

Most of the residents along Price Road were farmers; that was an obvious fact because the acreage of crops extended further than the eye could see in any direction. Since the days of Sir Walter Raleigh, nearly half of all the tobacco produced in the United States was produced in North Carolina. Many of the contributors to that acclaim lived on Price Road. Sometimes only the roof of a house was visible from the main road because it was surrounded by crops of tobacco. The farmers also raised an assortment of fruit and vegetable produce for their personal use: corn, string beans, chick peas, greens, tomatoes, peanuts, all varieties of melons, and anything else that they could utilize to eat, barter, or sell.

Those tillers of the soil, who planted and harvested their crops every year, had a deep appreciation and comprehension of nature's powers. The farmers depended on the reliability of the rise of the sun and the moon, the fall of the rain, and the change of the seasons; moreover, they were not ashamed to give praise to God - the supreme power that they acknowledged as the greatest artist of all. The farmers considered the landscape as a living canvas; they recognized the value of the wild flowers that instinctively found their way onto God's earthly canvas and created dabs of color in every unattended place. It was proof that things grew on this land - with or without a human helping hand.

The people along Price Road were hard workers, for the most part, struggling through life without the benefit of many modern conveniences. Newer farming tools and techniques that were commonly used throughout other parts of North Carolina and the South were not, for some reason, adapted as quickly in this region. Although almost all the people along Price Road made their living as farmers, the methods they used were the same as the previous generation - with very minute changes. It was as if time held it's breath as it passed over Price Road. Even the modern conveniences, such as indoor plumbing [toilets and running water], electricity, and telephones escaped most homes on this countryside until just a few years ago. However, the people didn't grumble about their lack of modern conveniences; they simply made do with what they had and could afford, without complaining.

The old folks said, *"No need to worry yourself into a frizzy about something if there is nothing you can do about it."*

In 1865 the Freedman's Bureau, created out of the War Department's American Freedman's Inquiry Commission, was responsible for the distribution among the ex-slaves for up to 850,000 acres of southern land - which was confiscated or abandoned pursuant to the civil war. *Forty acres and a mule* was the slogan for the short-lived Reconstruction land grant program that was responsible for the ex-slaves acquisition of much of the farmland along Price Road. In many cases it was the descendants of those slaves who owned and still farmed the land they inherited from their fathers and grandfathers.

However, some of the less fortunate Negro farmers lived in a sharecrop arrangement; others were renters. Many of those families were descendants of ex-slaves who could not escape the Peonage system, a legal enforcement of slave-like labor in the South, which was in place after the Civil War and well into the 1900s. When the Peonage system was law, the ill-fated Black person, who was caught on the street, could be jailed as a *vagrant* and fined. Then, the fine was paid by a White plantation owner whose previous free work-force was lost due to the Emancipation Proclamation. The plantation owner was then legally entitled to use the imprisoned *vagrant* for hard labor every day, and lock him up every night, until the judge determined the debt was paid. The Peonage system was really harsher on the Negro than being a slave because he/she was no longer a valued piece of property; consequently, kindness, consideration, and care did not exist. The captured Peon became a disposable being - worth less than a pet cat or dog.

The Sharecrop system was established to fill in the economical gaps for the White landowners; it was yet another legalized way to rip-off the ex-slaves. At any rate, many of the Black families on Price Road still bore the residue of those systems; some were still caught in the sharecrop system, and some were still labeled as Peons because they were poor. The Black community along Price Road enveloped all of these families, and they all knew each other although a social stratification existed.

Since the Civil War ended, it was a prevailing custom for friends and neighbors, on Price Road, to co-venture with their crops by helping each other at each developmental stage, from planting the crop, through the harvest, the curing, and taking the final yield to market. Neighboring families, Black and White, worked together in each others fields: they ate at the same table, drank from the same dipper at the well, they sweated together, and did whatever was necessary to harvest a crop that was sufficient to provide each family with enough food and money to exist throughout the winter. The necessity for survival seemed to eliminate the division of skin color between the poor share cropping families. There was no apparent separation of the Black farmer or White farmer in the tobacco fields along Price Road - at least during the times when they needed each other's help.

The choice of jobs in and around Leaksville was limited for Negroes. The well-to-do White families, who lived in town, hired some of the Colored women from Price Road as housekeepers, nannies, laundresses, and cooks. It was almost expected that a young person, from the Black community, would leave Leaksville for better job opportunities as soon as they could; they usually did not return, except to visit, or until they were old and ready to retire - if then. However, as long as they had friends and family members who still lived there, those transplanted 'Tar Heels' continued to call Leaksville '*home*'. Many of the family members who remained at 'home' were older adults, and their grandchildren, nieces, and nephews came to spend the summer every year.

The female servants, who were employed by the White townsfolk, still worked on their own families' farm. These women rose before day-break to clean, cook, and do the laundry for their own families; then, they went to the White woman's home to do the same for the White family. When the maids came back to their farmhouses, at the end of their regular workday, they continued to work late into the night at those same chores as they prepared for the next day. All of the major housework along Price Road, including cooking, was done on Saturday even when it was harvest time and there was an abundance of work to be done in the fields. Still, a farmer would never be seen at work on his farm on a Sunday – God's day. That would be blasphemy! Sunday was a day for worship and rest <u>only</u>.

THE CHURCH LADIES

All the women shared an exhausted feeling of 'a *woman's work is never done.'* They toiled laboriously through the drudgery of their everyday life; nevertheless, even if they were tired, most of those mothers still took their children to church on Sunday mornings. The little girls wore Shirley Temple curls and Vaseline shined patent leather shoes, and the little boys were spit and shined as best as could be.

The men were supportive in the church, but the women were the real foundation of the congregation. A few of the Negro families on Price Road, who lived close to the Leaksville city limits sign, attended the Wesley African Methodist Episcopal Church (AME), a neat red brick 'city' church on Henry Avenue. The majority of Negro families on Price Road went to either Spring Baptist Church, on Price Road, Grace Baptist Church – near Stoneville, or Hope Methodist Church, a smaller country church with white wood siding, located on Shady Grove Road - a few miles from the Price Road intersection. Each church was surrounded by a graveyard. The members of the church buried their deceased on church grounds or on a remote section their family's property.

Although limited in number, a few Black people actually moved back *'home'* after they traveled to other parts of the world, served in the armed services, attended school in the North, or retired from their life's work; therefore, some of the residents, along Price Road, had experienced a small piece of their lives outside the jurisdiction of the demeaning Jim Crow laws. Many of these returning citizens had been introduced to the Catholic faith in Philadelphia, New York, Boston, Chicago, or at least above the Mason Dixon line; however, the one Catholic Church in Leaksville, like all other churches in the south, was segregated. White Christians did not openly admit that they were segregationist while their actions substantiated the fact that indeed they were.

"The hour of church service, from 11o'clock to 12 o'clock, on Sunday morning is the most segregated time of the week." a very observant person once said.

In fact, many of the White legislators, who were responsible for the Jim Crow laws and the Peonage laws, professed to be 'born again' Christians. Therefore, Leaksville's Black population attended their own Baptist, Methodist, or Pentecostal [Holiness] Churches on Sunday mornings. Policies of segregation continued to constrain all citizens over the United States: sometimes in very subtle ways, sometimes very overt ways, even after death, even into their segregated grave sites. Leaksville, NC was a microchip that reflected the moral and racial climate throughout the United States.

When she was a teenager Rozlyn Berry, whose family lived on Price Road, once asked, "Are there two heavens?" No one could answer her question...

Church was a place to worship, but it was also a place to socialize. The church service always started with a sing and praise warm-up. Melodies of soulful yearnings were led by worship leaders with the rhythmic punctuation of tambourines and hand clapping.

"I'll learn to trust in Jesus, [clap]
I'll learn to trust in God, [clap]
Through it all, [clap] through it all," [clap]

Pastor Johns, the pastor of the Spring Baptist church on Price Road, was also a farmer. The small congregation couldn't afford to pay anyone to be a full time preacher; in fact, Pastor Johns sometimes accepted his weekly stipend in the form of a chicken, or a bushel of potatoes. His days were confined to his farm work and the work of the church. Although he was not theologically trained, just a man who heard God's call, Pastor Johns was a dedicated servant who was determined to be the backbone of God's church and to attend to God's flock. He worked around the clock toward that purpose, and his sermons were full of fire and brimstone.

"I don't want to get to the pearly gates and have Saint Peter tell me that one soul didn't get into heaven because I didn't make that person understand the consequences of sin." Pastor Johns told his congregations – there were two.

The Pastor alternated his Sundays between two country churches; Grace Baptist Church (near Stoneville) on the first and third Sundays, and Spring Baptist Church (on Price Road) on the second and fourth Sundays. The congregations remained at church all day and ate delicious potluck dinners between worship services. The membership at each church was almost interchangeable because those with transportation visited the alternate church often, and they shared programs and special events - such as: the Xmas and Easter programs, and homecoming picnics.

The Homecoming was an event that family and friends, who no longer lived in the area, returned to Price Road every year to attend. Even husbands who didn't usually attend church functions came to the *Homecoming;* it was an occasion that supercharged everyone with excitement from the moment the annual date was announced. A good time was always guaranteed.

The most recent shared event was the annual 'Tom Thumb Wedding', sponsored by the usher boards of both churches. It was a building fundraiser that the usher board had held for the past fifteen years. In fact, almost every church activity was used to raise money for the building fund. The entire miniature wedding party was composed of little children dressed up in colorful crepe paper outfits. The mothers worked together to design the costumes by tucking, puckering, and stretching the crepe paper into incredible original creations. Little four year old Heather Shaw married six year old Vartan Berry in the Tom Thumb wedding one year. The church women whispered to each other behind their handheld fans. They were middle aged women who giggled like school girls as they predicted a possible real life relationship between the two youngsters.

"Bet they grow up and really get married to each other"

"They are so cute together."

The following year two other children were the focus of the church ladies prophecies. Anyone who listened to the church ladies entertain themselves, through the programming of their children, would believe that marriage was the fundamental goal of adulthood; surprisingly, those same women were not happy in their own married lives. Yet, they continued to perpetuate the teaching, via the Tom Thumb Wedding, that they heard all of their lives… *Boys and girls should look forward to marriage.*

Rozlyn Berry was an inquisitive and observant child. Rozlyn always hung around the adults; she was like the dust in the air, always in the atmosphere, but not noticeable until the dust settled. She listened to the church ladies' joyful backstage utterances at the Tom Thumb Weddings, and she watched the same women sob and cry uncontrollably at authentic weddings.

Rozlyn's gut instincts warned her that the church ladies knew what the unsuspecting bride was really getting into. Subsequently Rozlyn, even though she was very young, surmised that the church ladies cried at real-life weddings because they felt sorry for the bride. Rozlyn thought it was in the vein of *'misery loves company'* because the church ladies still pushed and pushed all the young church girls…

"How old are you girl? When you going to get married?"

"If you don't get married soon nobody is going to want you."

"Don't let the men know how smart you are, you'll never get married then!"

Whenever Rozlyn thought of the *church ladies*, she thought of snakes in the grass with split tongues. They were four middle aged women who held important clerical positions at the church: the Sunday school supervisor, president of deaconess board, president of the pastor's aide committee, and the church secretary. They were the women who needed the congregation to honor them because of their important church positions, which they held for a lifetime - or until they were ready to retire because of old age or illness. No-one in the congregation dared to suggest that either job be done by a different person.

Pastor Johns realized that the church ladies were bold and sometimes abrasive in the interpretation of their beliefs, but they were also his biggest helpers; he could depend on them to get whatever task had to be done in the basic week to week operations of the church. That was the reason Pastor Johns did not attempt to control the church ladies' "holier-than-thou" attitude, which was almost always offensive. He needed them even though it was because of the church ladies that Pastor Johns' private conversations with God were so lengthy.

The church ladies were always willing to do church work, they were leaders; in fact, they formed a church based club, *The Willing Workers...* It was their special God blessed elite clique. On Sundays the four members of The Willing Workers Club wore the most jeweled, feathered, and flowered hats in the congregation; therefore, they were always the most conspicuous ladies in church.

The church ladies seemed to think on one accord: they discussed the other members of the congregation daily, they made joint decisions, they were alert for signs of back-sliders, without solicitation they personally advised members of the church about God's spiritual expectations, and they developed strategies designed to help their fellow parishioners to become better Christians. The church ladies even developed a list of rules for holy and sanctified Christian living, which they tried to personally enforce, in order to help the sinners of the congregation get into heaven.

- Do not listen to the radio except for religious programs.
- Do not do any housework on Sunday.
- Do not play games on Sundays that include jumping or running.
- No dancing or card playing.
- All contact with the opposite sex must be chaperoned until age 21.
- Ladies, do not wear skirts higher than 12" above the floor.
- Be kind to others, so when you die people will come to your funeral.
- Do not visit Black Bottom [a group of homes, extending from Price Road, where the people who live there are considered as Peons and sinners by the righteous church ladies]
- Gentlemen must wear jackets and ties in church, and women must wear stockings, gloves, and hats in church. Weather does not offer an excuse.

The church ladies said... *Then said Jesus, Father, forgive them: for they know not what they do."* Luke 23: 34

And every day Pastor Johns prayed, "God please give me the strength to work with your Willing Workers."

Ever since she was a teenager Rozlyn Berry was aware that the church ladies were much more vested at digging through the detritus of sin in other parishioner's homes than they were in controlling the atmosphere within their own homes.

Rozlyn discovered, throughout years of watching and listening, that each church lady had her own closet of concealed personal secrets... Each lady's private internal closet was crammed full of secrets locked behind the complex doors of the church lady's closed, non-accepting mind. Whenever a church lady's husband stumbled into her bed at dawn, smelling of whiskey, she would simply prepare breakfast and tell the children, "Your father is sick this morning, don't make any noise... Sit down and eat your breakfast; then, get your chores done – quietly."

A church lady always held her head high, without expression, whenever one of her children came home from school and told her, "There is this kid in my class who has the same last name as me, and everybody says he looks just like me."

A church lady would send her unmarried daughter off to a relative to live for awhile, only to have that daughter return home in a few months with a baby that, "We adopted." Or perhaps the baby would be, "A niece or nephew" - an unnamed sister or brother's child that, "We gonna take care of for awhile."

A church lady learned early in her marriage to store her change purse in the security of her bra (her breast bank), or to sleep with it under her pillow. She became creative in places to hide her savings or tithe money; places such as: the hem of window drapes, pouches pinned into the waistlines of pink snuggies or cotton slips, or even envelopes taped to the underbelly of the metal head of the sewing machine. The hiding place had to be a place no-one would think of looking, a place her husband or children would not find. Such creativity was necessary because even in the privacy of a church lady's home it was not safe to leave money unguarded; husbands and children stole from wives, mothers, or grandmothers and then feigned complete innocence. The church ladies learned early in their marriages that the best way to avoid a confrontation about missing money was to keep it from becoming missing – keep it in a secret place.

The denial of their own reality gave the church ladies an enormous amount of time to invest their initiatives into other people's spiritual lives. Therefore, based only by their own determination, the church ladies were proficient and skilled at maneuvering in and out of other people's private business as they felt it related to the salvation of ones' soul; not necessarily their own.

Rozlyn didn't listen to the church ladies. Instead, as soon as she was old enough, she left her family's home on Price Road to pursue her education and career. She never wanted to be caught down on the farm barefoot and pregnant. It was an anxiousness Rozlyn felt in her core but could not express, not even to her mother. She felt an inner strength, a need for independence and adventure; therefore, when Rozlyn Berry went to Washington D.C., to attend Howard University, she knew that she would never return to Price Road to live - only to visit. With Rozlyn gone, every Sunday the church ladies questioned her mother, Mrs. Berry.

"When is Rozlyn going to settle down and get married?"

"It's going to be hard for her to catch a husband with her college education."

"Rozlyn needs to get married and give you some grandchildren before she gets too old."

"Nobody's going to want to marry her when she gets too old."

Then the church ladies pressed their pale lips together, pulled their long full skirts over their crossed knees, and adjusted their flower covered hats to just the right angle, and without missing a beat they sang…

"We'll understand it better bye and bye"… [clap]

THE OLD FOLKS

Everyday Ed stopped at the McNeil's store to: relax a little, buy gas and a bottle of pop, and hob-nob with the '*Old Folks*.' A large red metal Coca Cola container sat on one side of the front porch of the small store. On the opposite side of the porch sat four old men who had become an expected sight at the store by noon every day. Locals referred to the seemly diverse group as '*The Old Folks*' with all the respect that their age and life experience deserved. It was Ed's routine to: slide the top of the Coca Cola container open, to dig his arm down - through the ice to his elbow, to retrieve a chocolate Yoohoo soda-pop, and to nod his head as a respective acknowledgment of each of the old men.

"Howdy, Mr. Sycamore, Mr. Silas, Mr. Udell, Mr. Vera, nice day isn't it?" Ed O'Reilly always said to the garrulous, yet gallant, old friends who gathered at the McNeil store every afternoon. They relaxed in their favorite chairs on the front porch, sharing: big and tall stories, insight, and the wisdom of life they accumulated through experience and observation. Sometimes they played cards (usually Poker or Bid Whist.) Sometimes their conversations lingered over a game of checkers.

All four men were retired farmers. They always wore clean and pressed bib front blue jean coveralls, starched and pressed shirts, and large straw hats - which were sometimes used as a fan. As the four old friends sat in a semicircle on the porch of the country store, Ed imagined them as models on a large colorful poster advertising uniforms for retired farmers.

Mr. Sycamore, whose full head of thick wavy hair was still not completely gray, was the oldest of the group; he referred to the others as 'babies' because they were four, five, and seven years younger than he was.

"As far as I can 'member." Mr. Sycamore said while he rocked deliberately slow in his favorite cushioned, white wicker, rocking chair, "I was born four years after the civil war ended. Was that in1865? So, I was born in 1869."

Mr. Sycamore left it for someone else to calculate how old that made him every year; his unblemished caramel complexion, high check bones and thick wavy hair gave a hint to his Native American ancestry – but not his age. It was hard to determine Mr. Sycamore's age by his appearance.

"You know brown and black skin don't crack." Mr. Sycamore said with a chuckle directed toward his lighter skin buddies. He nodded his head for conformation from Mr. Udell, whose complexion was several shades darker than his own. The two shared a mutual assurance… "That's a fact!" they laughed.

Mr. Sycamore and his wife lived in the house on the lot next to the place where Mr. Ashford and his family used to live. Mr. Ashford, affectionately known as *Uncle DaDa*, was his only living nephew, his sister's son. If anyone looked close enough, they could see the loneliness on Mr. Sycamore's face. There was an empty space in Mr. Sycamore's life that could only be filled by his beloved nephew's presence, but a few years ago Mr. Ashford (Uncle DaDa), his wife, and grandchildren left Price Road. Mr. Sycamore didn't move with them because he didn't want to leave his home, but he had to admit that his senior years were not what he expected them to be… His wife was the only immediate family Mr. Sycamore had in North Carolina any more, but he thanked God for his friends at the store…

Mr. Vera, whose first name was Aloe, usually sat in the chair next to Mr. Sycamore. One of Mr. Aloe Vera's ancestors came to the United States from Yuan Jiang, a small town in China. Because of the racial blending in his family, Mr. Aloe Vera's physical appearance hardly gave any indication to his Chinese heritage. Aloe Vera was the shortest of the group of old folks; his 5'4" slim frame appeared to be rather fragile, yet he seemed to be more energetic than any of his friends. His rocking chair was always in constant motion; in fact, every day, rather than walk to the store, Mr. Vera jogged the mile and half from his house.

Mr. Vera was a natural health enthusiast; he was very familiar with herbs and nutrition. "Diet is vitally important to good health." Mr. Vera said. He was sixty-eight years old, and he couldn't remember the last time he was sick. Mr. Vera gave anyone, willing to listen, suggestions of cures to common maladies.

"I have been taking that for years, and I never get a cold." Mr. Vera said when he suggested Apple Cider Vinegar or Green Tea for just about every illness or potential illness.

"You have to understand the Ying and Yang balance of your body in order to keep from getting sick." Mr. Vera advised.

"Western doctors are not that many years away from cutting hair, blood letting, and prescribing leaches for cures to illnesses while Homoeopathic medicine has centuries of successfully documented remedies." he continued.

Mr. Vera raised a garden of herbs such as: Echinacea, garlic, Burdock root, Catnip, Buchu, Chamomille, and Dandelions. There were days when Mr. Sycamore and Mr. Vera had lively discussions about health and nutrition. Those were not debates, but more of a lively exchange of information because they supported the same agenda. Uncle DaDa was a valuable contributor to those discussions before he moved. Even though Uncle DaDa was younger than any of the 'old folks' they all followed suit with the rest of the Price Road community; Mr. Ashford was also their beloved Uncle DaDa, and Mr. Vera missed those conversations with Uncle DaDa…

Once when Mr. Silas was sick with the flu, he looked up from his feverish brow and saw the three health advocates at his bedside. Mr. Silas ended up with three different solutions for his illness. Since he didn't want to offend any one of his friends, Mr. Silas took all three treatment remedies.

"I figured - if it didn't kill me, it might cure me." Mr. Silas told the crowd at the store regarding his friendship cure-surge; of course, that was after he recovered, and felt like joking again.

Mr. Silas, who stood about 5'7", once had a head full of blond hair; however, it was mostly gone from the top of his head while in the back of his head the strands of hair, still struggling for attention, hung as a long mane toward his shoulders. Mr. Silas spoke extra loud, and he ignored any suggestion that he get a hearing exam.

"Man, will you stop talking so loud, we can hear you." his friends often said to him.

"Did you say something?" Mr. Silas always answered with a mock questioning look, "I can't hear you." Then there was laughter… It didn't take much for those friends to share laughter.

Mr. Silas was Lily McNeil's father; he and his wife, of fifty years, lived about a half mile down the road from the store - in the same house where Lily McNeil grew up. By the White folk's economic standards of the day, Mr. Silas' family was considered as poor white trash; he worked as a sharecropper most of his life. When Lily and Bo inherited the store from Bo's father, Lily was able to help her parents buy the land they had lived on for so many years. Mr. Silas looked forward to spending his afternoons at the store with his old friends; it was like a second home because his daughter and grandsons were around all day.

The fourth member of the 'old folks' quartet was Mr. Udell who lived down the road a-piece with his daughter, Daisy, her husband and son - Briar (Mr. Udell's only grandson). Taree Udell, Mr. Udell's son, lived nearby. Taree was not married, and as far as Mr. Udell knew his son had not given him any grandchildren. Taree Udell was the owner of the Meadow Woods Night Club, an upscale entertainment spot located at the end of Price Road, near Stoneville. Because of Taree's successful nightclub business, the entire Udell family was well known throughout Rockingham County. As Ed ambled closer to the four men, Mr. Udell was telling a story about his nine year old grandson, Briar.

"Briar was pretending he had a water gun, running around squirting water all over the dog. His mother noticed the commotion, and saw that the boy was squirting the water out of a red rubber bag with a long tube - with a white tip. Water was coming out of all the holes on the end whenever he aimed it at the dog and released the metal clip on the long tube. Well, they were running around the front yard like crazy with this thing - squirting water all over the place. My daughter, Daisy, had a fit! She ran after Briar, grabbed him by the neck, and beat the holy hell out of him with a wet dishrag." Mr. Udell said.

"Oh Lord!" Mr. Silas interjected. "You ain't been whipped - until you been dishrag whipped." He said as he put up his arms to dodge an imaginary, yet remembered, dishrag attack. Mr. Silas's movement brought forth laughter and *Amen's* from the group of seniors.

"At first I didn't understand the problem; then, I realized <u>what</u> Briar was using to squirt the water." Mr. Udell continued

"I couldn't let Daisy see me laugh, so I went back into the house. Briar had taken her douche bag off the hook on the back of her door; he had no idea what it was, and she didn't tell him 'cause he's too young to understand. And 'cause he a boy - you know what I mean? Briar knew he had no business touching anything that wasn't his. Poor thing, he just cried... I mean his mother really put a whipping on him!" Mr. Udell said. The old friends couldn't stop laughing while Mr. Udell described the event; it took a minute before Mr. Udell could compose himself enough to continue...

"Later I asked Briar why he did that. He told me that he had seen his mother put water in the bag and squirt water out of its tip, so he figured it would make a fun water pistol; then, Briar asked me why the tip had a funny smell to it. It dawned on me that he must have thought he had the hot water bag. Both bags look alike, except for the long tube, I mean they are both red rubber, and both hold water; it's a natural mistake the boy made... You know, I bet he don't make that mistake again, he'll find out soon enough what that was he was playing with, and why it smelt so funny." Mr. Udell concluded.

The four 'old folks' laughed together along with a few customers who stopped to listen to the story. Ed joined in the laughter, he had to admit it was a funny story; any mischievous boy could have easily made the same mistake. The boy, in his youthful fantasy, '*assumed*' how the red bag could be used. Ed thought about Briar - the poor kid. Ed wondered how long it would take Briar to learn a life lesson he had come to understand... In life you can't *assume* anything.

The old folks said... "*To assume is to make an **Ass** out of **U** and **Me**.*"

The old folks also said... "*One's perspective changes depending on where they stand – how high up life's mountain they have climbed.*"

The old folks said... "*Enjoy the days of the sweet innocence of childhood because that time is limited.*"

The church ladies said... "*Train up a child in the way he should go, and he will not depart from it.*"

21

Ed's time spent with the Old Folks was always a high point of his workday. He learned from their wisdom, enjoyed their humor, and sometimes even contributed to their noontime conversation.

*   *   *

Every workday started the same for Ed O'Reilly; he arrived at seven AM every morning at the small post office on Monroe Street in Leaksville. He organized the mail into his bag, and drove down Washington Street - Leaksville's main street and shopping district. The sleepy downtown street yawned and stretched itself to come awake, corresponding with the beginning of Ed's workday. Ed saw: the people as they changed shifts at the hotel on the corner of Monroe and Washington Streets, groups of friends as they hurried from the local bus station and rushed to hit the time clock at the Belks Department Store. Ed waved to acquaintances on their way to work at the Colonial Food Market, or down the road to the Duke Power Company. He waited at a red light as the scheduled Greyhound bus left the bus station on Bridge Street and turned in front of him. He drove down Center Church Road, pass Douglas High and Elementary School - Leaksville's Colored school. At seven forty-five AM every day Ed passed the Weeping Willow tree in the front yard of Rose's Hair Salon where the Colored women got their hair done. Less than two minutes later he reached the Leaksville city limits sign. Within a minute Ed's mail car approached the Hilltop and Black Bottom mailboxes; as usual, observers could set their watches by him.

HILLTOP AND BLACK BOTTOM

All of the women on Price Road were not church ladies; some went in the opposite direction. Many hung out every weekend at the Hilltop Night Club. It was a long, narrow, black building, with a red metal roof which didn't look too different from a long barn; in fact, Hilltop Night Club was originally a tobacco storage barn.

Price Road began at the city limits sign by the small bridge over Matrimony Creek; it made a very slight curve as it followed an incline before it became the major passageway through the rural farmlands. As an offshoot from the curve, on the left side of the road, a wide dirt space expanded into a large parking lot in front of the Hilltop Night Club. On Friday and Saturday nights, the parking lot was always packed with people hanging in and out of the assorted cars, ready to party hard. Lively music and strong corn liquor flowed in and out of the long black building with the red metal roof... That's when the young women dressed for a festive occasion, and the smooth and suave young men displayed their charm and rippling muscles as they tried to romance a lady – any lady - for the evening. They had heard that girls up North considered southern country boys to be good lovers; therefore, the young men who partied at Hilltop considered it an honor to be called *country* because they felt it was a term that accentuated the positive - they thought of themselves as 'players.' After all, they understood nature in every form... As farmers, they spent their days involved in some way with nature's reproduction system; hence, it was a natural extension for the farmer to truly understand human sexuality.

"Come on woman - let me take you home tonight. I know how to make you feel good." the self-assured 'country' player said as he cuddled the female objective for the evening. Generally those young stallions felt that the local southern girls should consider themselves as lucky; after all, those girls should appreciate the fact that the world's best lovers were the men in their own back yard. That was not a cocky attitude; it was just a statement of fact...

The stress and sore muscles the young farm hands accumulated throughout a week of hard work were relieved every weekend through the combination of liquor, music, and raunchy dancing. The coarse wood dance floor at Hilltop reverberated with a soulful beat under the red and blue light bulbs as the music inspired individualistic versions of the Bop, the Huck-a-buck, and the slow Grind. Any passerby could hear the enticing sounds of Sam Cooke, Ray Charles, Etta James, and Ike and Tina Turner blasting from the jukebox.

The church ladies warned the church members… *"Never let yourself be caught in that 'Devil's Den of Iniquity'."*

* * *

The cluster of five houses, built in the gully, on the dirt road that ran in the back of Hilltop Night Club was known as 'The Black Bottom.' If the homes were in a plusher neighborhood it would have been designated as a *Cul-de-sac,* instead, it was just a dead-end dirt road. Most of the people who lived in Black Bottom were related.

The one exception was 'Miss Hag' who just rode into 'Black Bottom', one day long ago, on a horse with its tail knotted and tied with fancy ribbons. No-one on Price Road, or in Black Bottom, had ever seen the strange lady before. Miss Hag just appeared and made herself a home in the old abandoned one room cinder block building, deep into the grove of trees, accessible only by a winding narrow path on the edge of Black Bottom.

Miss Hag wore her hair in dred-locks that were so long that she could twist most of the dreds into a turban - made entirely of her own hair. The hair style fascinated everyone; it looked as if obedient snakes took residence atop her head. One day the brazen children in the Bottom asked Miss Hag how she got her hair-turban to stay in place. That may have been the only personal question Miss Hag ever answered, for she actually took her hair down to show them.

No-one knew her real name, and she never said what it was; therefore, the adults followed the children's lead and began to call the stranger 'Miss Hag'. She didn't tell them anything different, so the name stuck. 'Miss Hag' lived alone. When she interacted with her Black Bottom neighbors, it was with a quiet distance - an exchange that was

24

mostly unspoken dictate. Despite her apparent disregard for modern standards, customs, and fashions, Miss Hag stood, sat, and walked with an impressive regal attitude: her head and neck erect, her back straight, and her walk graceful.

'Black Bottom' had a reputation; it was known as a place to hang out. The religious people around Price Road viewed it as a sacrilegious place, and refused to let their children befriend the children who lived in the Bottom. Of course total contact with the children from the Bottom could not be entirely eliminated because all of the Black children, from the Leaksville community, went to the same school.

There were lots and lots of children to be fed and clothed in Black Bottom; nobody wore shoes until the ground was covered with snow. Children in some of the families attended school on alternate days because they had to share their shoes. It was a common joke that there are so many children living in 'Black Bottom' that the quarters could have its own intramural football, basketball, or baseball games, and there would still be enough children left over to be the spectators. At school the classmates taunted and teased the children from the 'Bottom', singing,

> *"There was an old lady, who lived in the Bottom*
> *Had so many children, she didn't know what to do.*
> *Rumor was there were twenty-four.*
> *So, what did she do?*
> *She had some more..."*

The trees in the Bottom actually grew in a circular formation; their branches seemed to join together, like a canapé, high above the ground. The limbs of the trees were so close together that when it rained very little rainwater ever actually reached the ground directly from above.

Dry dust seemed to be the only thing in Black Bottom that grew in abundance; a heavy rainstorm always developed mini rivers that rippled quickly down into the gully, via the narrow dirt road that sprouted from Price Road. A violent flow of rainwater ran down the road and gathered in a giant puddle of mud, right in the middle of the circle of homes – underneath the canapé of trees, which also kept direct sunlight out of the Bottom. Whenever there was a hard rain, it was impossible to walk outside of the big circle of mud; people who lived in the

Bottom resigned themselves to the fact that they were going to have muddy feet. The standing brown mud-water lasted for several days after a storm because of the obstructed sunlight.

Black Bottom seemed to be the one spot along Price Road that God's artistry missed; his paint brush must have run out of the color green at that spot. The land in Black Bottom was not suitable for farming because nothing seemed to grow there. Actually, the name of the location could easily have been called 'Brown Bottom' since everything there was brown: brown dirt where there should have been green lawns, tall brown tree trunks topped with a canopy of unnatural brownish green leaves, brown houses with brown porches and dirty brown windows, and dozens of little dusty brown feet ran around under the brown tinted sheets (which at one time were white) – that were hung across stiff wire clotheslines. The only things colorful to be seen around Black Bottom were the small patches of wildflowers in the back of the lackluster houses.

Nevertheless, the residents of the Bottom banned together to form an alliance to solve their own problems – they used the little formal education they had. Every individual was full of self pride; they never asked anyone for charity even though their needs were great. Their higher education came from the life college of hard knocks. It was not the lifestyle the parents in Black Bottom would have chosen for themselves, or their children; nevertheless, while they told their children stories of hope, the adults did whatever they had to do in order to survive. Every weekend, when the weather permitted, the people who lived in Black Bottom hosted an all day open air jamboree; **everything** was for sale.

The weekend parties provided a weekly income to supply the bare necessities for the impoverished organizers. As strange as it seemed, violence was not something that usually occurred. Sometimes a patron might get a little drunk and want to start a fight; however, there were always strong young men around who were adept at defusing a dispute before it got out of hand.

Attendees came to Black Bottom looking for a roust-a-bout atmosphere; they expected to: eat ribs right off the grill, play craps at the corner of a house, partake of moonshine (straight out of the still), play cards (Bid Wisk, Spades, Poker, or Deuces Wild), or find a willing bed-mate in one of the houses with the red light bulb on the porch. Some party-goers even wandered down the path to the grove to see Miss Hag. She told their fortune by reading their palms or tea leaves; in fact, for a few dollars Miss Hag would even put a hex on someone.

Black Bottom came about its name because it was a place where only Black people lived. Nearby there was a wide gravel road, down Price Road a *little piece* from the Hilltop Night Club, which led directly up a knoll to a large brick house across Price Road. When slavery existed, the Plantation Master lived there; later it became the home of the Berry family, but it was still known as the 'Big House.' Rozlyn Berry grew up there, but like her brothers she was not sure of how her mother and father came to own the big house. Rozlyn heard other people talk about how Black Bottom was once the slave quarters, but those things were never discussed in the Berry's home. At any rate, the people who lived in Black Bottom were survivors; they ignored the fact that the church ladies never had anything to say to them.

Ed, the mailman, had never been down the dirt road to Black Bottom. He couldn't even see the cluster of houses from the highway. Since the mailboxes of the Black Bottom residents were lined up on Price Road, Ed only made a personal acquaintance whenever someone, who lived in the Bottom, was waiting for mail at their box.

That was how he met Nardu Hearst. The first day Ed and Nardu saw each other they both realized that they were not complete strangers; they had seen each other before. Both were inducted into service at the Army Intake Center on the same day back in 1941.

They recognized each other as being Leaksville residents. Because Negro and White recruits were separated, the two young frightened recruits did not actually speak to each other that day; nevertheless, the familiar face was acknowledged through a simple nod of the head and a nervous half smile - one to the other. There were questions each man would have asked the other if they could have; instead, each inductee stood silent as they stared at each other from opposite sides of the extremely crowded intake room.

Ed did not see Nardu again until many years after the war was over. Nardu was waiting at his mailbox one morning, and the two veterans began an honest and sincere friendship. They talked about everything - from raising flowers to politics. Sometimes they talked about their war experiences, but not often; that always seemed to be a difficult conversation.

Ed had enjoyed his service years, and he understood that he was fortunate to have come back home without being wounded. Nardu was not as lucky; he lost his right arm above the elbow while he was in the service, and he was not able to find a job when he returned home. Nardu was not able to help much on a farm as a hired hand since there was only a nub where his arm used to be. Nardu was aware of the reaction from most people when they saw his nub. When the weather was cool he wore a long sleeved shirt to cover his arm. In the warmer months long sleeves were just too hot to bear; therefore, Nardu endured the repulsion he experienced, especially from the children, whenever he wore short sleeved shirts.

Nardu grew up in Black Bottom; his father was arrested as a Peon a few months before Nardu was born. His father died, under mysterious circumstances, while at work under the Peon system; consequently, Nardu's mother was left pregnant and homeless. Her aunt, who lived in Black Bottom, took her in; consequently, Nardu was born in the Bottom - the child of a Peon.

His hard start in life did not stymie Nardu's dreams. As a teenager Nardu dreamed of: opening a barber shop when he finished his Army years, making good money, helping his family get out of Black Bottom, living in a nice home, and driving a shiny new Cadillac with a beautiful wife at his side.

Nardu actually developed competent barbering skills before he was drafted, and it didn't take long for his fellow recruits to learn of his abilities; hence, Nardu became the barber of the barracks. Cutting hair was Nardu's passion, and he worked hard to develop his skills; however, all of his haircutting dreams ended when he lost his arm. Instead of cutting hair, Nardu helped with his family's Black Bottom 'business' activities. Most times he tended the grill. As long as his food was good, Nardu's lack of an arm was not an issue in the Black Bottom family environment. But in spite of his survival instincts Nardu led a lonely life. He couldn't help feeling self conscious about his arm, so he was hesitant to pursue romance…

"The war waz'a lot of fun for me… I got to travel the world." Ed said to Nardu one day.

"Oh, I'm not talking 'bout the ones that got killed; I feel sorry for dose poor souls, but da rest of us, we had a hell ov'a good time! Running up dose hills, guns a blasting… I'm telling you it felt good… The way the adrenaline waz flowing!" Ed said.

"Well, 'weren't no happy time fo' me," Nardu interrupted sharply. "I spent my time either digging latrines or graves… or bagging bodies. Didn't loose my arm to no bullet, lost it 'cause I got'a cut that got infected… Couldn't get nothing to clean the cut with." Nardu said through clinched teeth. Ed started to speak, but some instinct checked him.

"Oh, we had'a first-aid kit. Didn't have much in it 'cept aspirin and alcohol… We poured a whole bottle of rubbing alcohol on my arm. Must not 'ave been strong enough… Ended up loosing it anyways!" Nardu said as he rubbed the end of his handicap.

"Hear tell the Colored soldiers actually go into combat now." Nardu continued. "The Buffalo Soldiers got'a combat team… the 370th Regiment. They went into Naples, Italy two years after I was discharged." Nardu said. His face took on a solemn countenance. After a reflective pause, Nardu inhaled deeply before he spoke again. During the moment of silence, Ed waited without comment; he didn't know what to say.

"Ma best friend died right 'fore I lost ma arm. He died 'cause he needed a transfusion…" Nardu continued. "He lost too much blood. White Medics wouldn't treat him. Said they wer't gonna touch no Nigga… He out there moving their dead bodies, 'n they don't want to touch him 'cause he Colored." Nardu said. His chest heaved as he struggled to snatch a breath that was running away.

"Besides they say they don't have no colored people's blood plasma, 'n there wer't no colored medics no-where 'round. My friend died… Didn't need to happen! In fact I didn't need to loose my arm; 'weren't no combat wound… Lost my best friend and my arm near-bout the same day… No sir, I went thru **Hell** o'va there. Ain't got no good memories fo' me!" Nardu said emphatically. Ed thought he saw tears swell in Nardu's eyes, but none fell.

Ed was stunned by what he heard from Nardu. Ed knew the United States Army was segregated. He knew there were separate units for the Black and White soldiers; still, he never focused on what that really meant before he talked to Nardu. Ed never knew any other way of life because he grew up in the Jim Crow South. Maybe he had just never given it much thought, but he honestly did not realize how those laws could be the cause of a fellow soldier's death; after all, they were all American soldiers: serving under the same flag, fighting for the same cause, for the same country. Ed and everybody he knew accepted the fact, without question, that the Jim Crow Laws were legal below the Mason Dixon Line; the United States courts and the President said so... Ed was speechless... He was only able to stare at Nardu while he tried to absorb the impact of Nardu's statements.

The more Ed talked to Nardu the more he learned about the impact of the segregation laws on non-White American citizens, and he began to slowly examine his own thinking and upbringing.

It was a beautiful spring day in 1950 when Ed and Nardu had that initial conversation; at the time, Ed was a thirty year old husband and father of two – a grown man. Yet, he felt a funny feeling brewing in the pit of his stomach; it was an unidentifiable hunger - as if he was just beginning a growth spurt. Ed began to look forward to his discussions with Nardu more and more... Questions... So many questions...

As Ed approached the cluster of mailboxes for Black Botom on his last day working on Price Road, he looked, with anticipation, to see if Nardu was waiting by the mailbox. He hoped so... Ed hoped to have at least one more by-the-mailbox conversation with Nardu.

The old folks said... "*Speak only the truth. Act with only the best intentions, once you get into the habit, you can live by this code.*

THE BERRY'S BIG HOUSE

The first home on the right side of the highway was a two story, five bedroom brick residence. The long wrap-around porch was framed by tall white Greek-like columns, which gave a look of affluence. The living room was spacious, and the dinning area could easily seat a dozen people. The back staircase, which led into the large kitchen, was originally used by the house slaves. Under the staircase was a small enclosed space, large enough to place a small cot. That was where the house slave, who worked as the 'Big-House' cook, slept. In the back of the house there was a large structure where the horses and carriages were kept before Henry Ford manufactured the automobile; after that, it was converted into a two car garage.

Just a few yards away from the 'Big house' sat a stationary, single width trailer mounted on cement blocks. The few multicolored morning glory flowers, on the side of the three front steps, bloomed only a few hours every morning. Ed appreciated the beauty the flowers offered as he began his work day. Seventy year old Mrs. Berry, Rozlyn's mother, lived alone in the trailer. Her husband, Woodward Berry, collapsed in the fields ten years earlier with massive heart failure. In order to help the aging Mrs. Berry her oldest child, Oran, with his wife and young children, moved back to the family home.

Mrs. Berry appreciated the comfort and kindness her son and his wife, Lora, gave her; their presence definitely lessened the actual pain that often gripped her stomach since the love of her life, Woodward, died. Mrs. Berry loved her four active grandchildren: Oran Junior, Daisy, and the twins Varda and Vartan – they were adorable. Still, as she grew older, Mrs. Berry realized how much she cherished her peace and quiet.

It was Mrs. Berry's suggestion that she purchase and move into a single width trailer, fifty yards away from the main house – alone. That way she could enjoy her grandchildren, and then go to the solitude of her own space - in her own home. Of course Mrs. Berry had to convince her son, who could not understand her reasoning, that the move was a good idea. Eventually, with Lora's help, Oran and Mrs. Berry reached a mutual decision; therefore, Oran and his family lived in the 'Big House' while Mrs. Berry lived in her trailer on the adjoining lot.

Mrs. Berry's deceased husband, Woodward, was a Herculean man who towered over his wife. Woodward Berry was not an unlikable man, but he was not formally educated; naturally, Mrs. Berry credited his lack of schooling for Mr. Berry's obvious deficiency in logic and reasoning. Sometimes Mrs. Berry was so frustrated because it was absolutely too difficult for her to get her husband to see the best solution to a problem; at times she felt as if she was holding onto a greased pig, something that could not be done easily. This personality trait was hard on his family because Woodward Berry made up his own mind about everything, and he did things his way - right or wrong. Mrs. Berry learned to accept his *I'm always right* attitude and lived with Woodward Berry for forty-five years, giving him three children: Oran, Rozlyn, and Woodward Jr.

Mrs. Berry truly loved her husband; moreover, she appreciated the fact that he was a church going man, that trait made his domineering personality bearable. When people asked her how she was able to stay happily married so long, Mrs. Berry never had a reply. She just smiled with slight twinkle in her eye, but she never actually said anything. It was only in the silence of her own solitude that Mrs. Berry repeated her favorite bible verse -.Psalm 27:14 - *Wait on the Lord: be of good courage, and he will strengthen thine heart: wait, I say, on the Lord…* God was the only one to hear.

Mrs. Berry used that verse to pray for the patience she needed in her marriage; it was her secret weapon, and it worked. In some ways her prayer worked so well that Mrs. Berry was sure she had generated a miracle. In his later years, Woodward became less stubborn and easier to get along with.

The church ladies said… *"The family that prays together stays together."*

It was a beautiful place; everybody always continued to identify it as 'The Big House', the name it was originally given when Black Bottom was known as 'Slave Row.' In fact, Plantation Road was still the name of the gravel road that led up the knoll, to the 'Big- House.' Oran Berry grew up in this beautiful house, yet he and his siblings did not know much about its history. When he was growing up, the adults did not share information about their business with their children; therefore, all Oran ever heard about their house was when he listened to his mother and father as they said their prayers at night. His parents always said, "Thank you God for our home." It was always apparent to the Berry children that their family had the nicest home on Price Road, so they also thanked God every night.

Oran Berry was tall and muscular. At almost fifty years old, his slightly gray hair gave him a distinguished appearance. His father, Woodward Berry, was a farmer. Oran never wanted to be a farmer; he had enough of working on a farm while he was growing up. When he was a child, Oran always added a secret request to his evening prayers.

"God, will you please make my life so I will never have to walk behind a plow again." he prayed.

Oran would rather scrub floors than dig in God's earth, pick tobacco, or shuck corn any day; he didn't even like to mow the lawn. Oran whispered his special request quietly into his folded hands since his appeal was only meant for God's ears; therefore, he knew it was a blessing from God when he found the custodial job at Fieldcrest Mills, a national manufacturer of linens and towels, which was originally the Marshall Field Company. Oran vowed to never complain no matter what happened at work, so every morning he said, "Thank you God!"

Oran's wife, Lora, was the housekeeper/cook for Richard and Mrs. Elizabeth McDonald. Mr. McDonald was the president of the Leaksville Bank; he and Mrs. McDonald owned most of the land still used for sharecropping along Price Road, and they didn't have any children. Lora felt it was a decent enough job; she did not feel fatigued at the end of her workday.

Oran's decision to move back home after his father died let his younger brother and sister, Woodward Jr. and Rozlyn, off the hook. They loved their mother dearly, but neither wanted the responsibility of their mother's care; they certainly didn't want to come back to Price Road to live. So, both Woodard Jr. and Rozlyn wrote often and sent money regularly; they were both so thankful to their older brother, Oran, for the reprieve.

"See yo gotta letter from Rozlyn... Hope she's doing good." Ed offered to Mrs. Berry whenever he recognized a letter was from Rozlyn. He remembered seeing Rozlyn in town when they were growing up. At that time, Ed did not know Rozlyn personally; he didn't even know her name. Ed was ten years old, and she appeared to be about his age. However, he was aware of the fact that the Colored girl couldn't go to the same school he did although he was not totally aware of why.

That was the point in his life that Ed really began to comprehend the fact that he should monitor his emotions, feelings, and vocalizations about Colored people. That realization came about because Ed mentioned to his classmate, Gorge Wallace, that he thought the girl, whose name he later learned was Rozlyn, was pretty.

"You don't need to think like that because that's a Nigga' gal! " Gorge erupted.

"What's wrong with'chu? Don't chu know nothing? She a Nigga! You can't think a Nigga is pretty, daz's too dark to be pretty!" Gorge yelled at Ed.

"I know daz's da truth 'cause both ma dad and granddaddy say so! Now, blond hair and blue eyes... Daz's what'chu call pretty!" Gorge said, pretending to be mesmerized as he pointed, with an exaggerated jester of approval, to a little White girl who was walking down the street.

Ed was stunned by Gorg's reaction, and he learned – right then and there - that he couldn't like a girl, or think she was pretty if she was colored. Still, Ed was confused. He remembered Ella, the lady who was his family's housekeeper and cook; he thought she was a pretty lady even if she was colored.

It was Ella who prepared his favorite meals, showed him how to tie his shoes, and brush his teeth; she even taught him how to fly a kite. Ella took care of all the children in his family from birth, and they loved her. No-one ever told him it was wrong when, as a child, Ed gave loving hugs and kisses to Ella. Even though the McNeil family was not wealthy, Ella worked for his parents until she died when

Ed was seven years old. Gorg's reaction to his statement about Rozlyn brought memories of Ella to the surface of Ed's mind, and he realized how much he missed her.

That was the pivotal day when Ed became very guarded about expressing his feelings and thoughts to other people. He was never sure his thoughts were acceptable, so he kept them imprisoned - locked behind the keyhole of his gaze. Ed became very observant, but not vocal. Still years later, Ed asked Mrs. Berry about her daughter, Rozlyn, every chance he got. He knew he was in love with his wife, Suellen, but that had nothing to do with it... Ed still thought: give praise where praise was due, truth was truth, and Rozlyn Berry was definitely a beautiful woman. And that was the truth as far as Ed was concerned.

After she graduated from Howard University, Rozlyn moved to New York; that was about the same time that Ed started to work on Price Road. Ed recognized Rozlyn's handwriting and return address on the envelopes of the weekly letters addressed to Mrs. Berry; it offered the perfect opportunity to inquire about her. Sometimes Mrs. Berry told him that Rozlyn, who was a lawyer now, was in: Paris, California, Canada, or Bermuda. Rozlyn might be anywhere. Throughout the years Rozlyn has worked for: Louis Martin (a not so well known Black counselor to presidents and a leader in the civil right's movement), the offices of the NAACP, and Congressman Adam Clayton Powell. In fact Ed thought he got a glimpse of Rozlyn on a televised news report about the Brown vs. The Board of Education lawsuit when the case was heard by the Supreme Court.

Ed continued to be a friend to Gorge throughout their high school years, but as they grew older their relationship became more of an acquaintanceship than a friendship. Ed heard that after his childhood friend, Gorge, was discharged from the Army he returned to Leaksville for only one visit. The rumor around town was that Gorge married a Colored woman he met in England, but he didn't bring his wife home to meet his family because his family did not approve of her. In fact, Gorge could not even ride through the state of North Carolina with his wife because mixed marriages were illegal. His father, Mr. Wallace, spewed vulgarities at his son as if he was demented; half the city of Leaksville could hear the old man's expletives...

"How dare ya marry a Nigga! Get outta here, 'n don't come back... Don't <u>ever</u> come back here!" Mr. Wallace roared as he threw a stone toward Gorge's back. Townspeople saw Gorge get on a Greyhound bus later that same day; he never came back to Leaksville, even when his mother died.

Ed smiled to himself as he thought... Gorge Wallace sure nuff changed his mind about beauty. Still, Ed couldn't help wondering if Gorge's wife was as pretty as Rozlyn Berry...

And the old folks said... *Our actions establish who we are, as much as who we are will establish our actions."*

* * *

"Morning Ed... How you doing today?" was the standard greeting from Old Mrs. Berry.

"Pretty good Mrs. Berry, if I say so myself... Here's yo mail... and Oran's too," was Ed's standard reply. Ed always placed the mail for both households directly into Old Mrs. Berry's hands.

"Ya'r flowers do look beautiful; ya must be sticking ya'r talented thumb 'n da ground ta make 'em grow so." he said.

"Why thank ya Mr. Ed. You sho-nuff know what to say to make a body feel good... See ya t'morrow... Same time, same place." Old Mrs. Berry always said as she started back up the driveway at a surprisingly fast pace for someone her age. Suddenly, she stopped in her tracks when she realized what day it was.

"Oh Ed, I won't see ya t'morrow will I?" Old Mrs. Berry said. Her voice could not conceal her disappointment.

THE EYE OF A NEEDLE

As Ed drove on toward the next group of mailboxes he passed a wide field of tall corn on both sides of the road. He knew the surrounding farmland belonged to Mr. Richard McDonald, the President of the Leaksville Bank, and his brother-in-law, Mr. Allan Ryan, a Leaksville City Councilman. In the old days, before the Emancipation Proclamation, the land was one large tobacco plantation owned by the Ryan family. After the slaves were freed, old man Ryan sold some of the land and converted the rest into a profitable share crop business; upon his death the Ryan estate was divided between his son, Allen Ryan – who was married to Sally, and his daughter, Elizabeth – who was married to Richard (Dick) McDonald.

A few small homes, made of wood, were hastily constructed on the property about seventy years ago; then, the structures were left to decay all those years – with little or no maintenance. Both men, Mr. McDonald and Mr. Ryan, are often verbally chastised by their wives about the massive amount of improvements that should be made to the almost non-livable shacks.

There wasn't anyone waiting for Ed at the Shaw and Parker mailboxes; everyone was hard at work in the fields. Ed's eyes narrowed as he tried to see the roofs of either the Shaw or the Parker homes over the top of the dense tobacco rows. Ed thought about the argument he heard spill outside the McDonald's home when he drove past their house earlier.

*   *   *

"Dick, you could fix the roof fo' dose people," Mrs. McDonald yelled "It would'nt hurt you!"

"Woman, le've me 'lone! Don't care bout no damm roof! dem Niggers ain't bring in 'nough crops last year ta pay fo' no new roof!" Richard McDonald retorted over his shoulder as he rushed toward the driveway.

"Den just repair it... Don't hav' ta be new... Do something 'fore winter... 'fore da whole house fall down!" Elizabeth McDonald pleaded as she stood in her pale blue chenille housecoat. Her arms were wrapped around one of the large columns on the large porch that surrounded the elegant two story brick home. Her voice had a particular whining resonance that gave everything she said a begging tone.

Mr. McDonald drove his new Mercedes Benz hastily out of the horseshoe driveway in the front of his home. He sped pass the stone gate post, the exclamation point to the three foot high stone wall, which separated the McDonald property from the rest of the city; he was in a hurry to get away from that woman!

"Always nagging... Why can't she be satisfied? I provide good fo her; she haz a nice home... Why does she have ta spend her time worrying 'bout them people? They ain't no kin to her!" Richard McDonald muttered to himself as he drove away quickly.

Mr. McDonald boldly played the strong male role in his house. He followed the lessons he learned from his father, grandfather, and uncles. By their example, his male role models taught Richard (Dick) McDonald, and his brothers, how to treat a wife and colored folk; consequently, Dick McDonald didn't care if the roof leaked. He was not going to spend his money on anything for those folks. "And, the Parkers - I know daz White, but daz poor just like da Niggra's! Ain't no need in dis world for'a White man to be poor - so I ain't caring nothing 'bout them neither!" Dick McDonald yelled out at the molecules in the air, for no-one was there to hear him while he drove to the Leaksville Bank – alone.

Mr. McDonald sat for a minute in the parking lot of the bank before he went in to deal with the pile of work on his desk; he needed to get a grip on his emotions. He had given himself a headache again because of his primal reaction to his wife's suggestion. As Dick sat in his car, in the reclusive silence of his own mind, his secret thought resurfaced - without his permission - a thought he never spoke aloud.

Dick McDonald thought... The Colored people sho'nuff have some pretty women! Abruptly he closed his eyes - so tight that his head ached even more; it was as if he was afraid his secret thoughts could seep out through the sockets of his eyes. Dick raised his left hand to massage his brow, and he noticed the old circular scar at the base of his little finger. The sight of his scared hand brought flashes of something, from the past, into Dick's mind's eye… He squeezed his eyes together tighter… The headache… OH – THE HEAD ACHES! The employees at the Leaksville Bank looked out of the window, and they wondered why it was taking Mr. McDonald so long to get out of his car…

Elizabeth McDonald went pensively back into her house. She just couldn't understand her husband or her brother's attitudes. She knew they could afford the repairs to the sharecropper's houses. What was wrong with her husband's thinking? Elizabeth pondered the facts: Dick went to church every Sunday; he heard the preacher read from the Bible whatever it said about how you should do unto others like you want them to do unto you; yet, Dick didn't seem to think that poor people were human too?

"I'm afraid Richard ain't going to make it into heaven." she reflected aloud to herself, unaware that anyone heard. Lora Berry was washing the breakfast dishes; she never looked up, but she heard every word that Mr. and Mrs. McDonald screamed at each other. Lora knew Mrs. McDonald well enough to realize that her boss was on a mission, and somehow the sharecropper's houses were going to get the roofs - with or without Mr. McDonald's knowledge.

Elizabeth McDonald went into her bedroom to get dressed. There was a quiet determination about her movements as she prepared to go to her brother's house. She needed Sally's help to solve this problem. Elizabeth and Sally were secretly reading the Bible, and praying directly to God for salvation. Their husbands had no idea that the women were involved in such serious discussions; they did not know that the major portion of Elizabeth and Sally's days were spent studying the Bible, and praying overtime for their husbands. If Richard and Allen knew about the daily Bible discussions their wives were embracing, they might have felt the need to monitor or oversee Elizabeth and Sally's scriptural understanding.

"We been blessed with riches; we must help our brethren who have not been so blessed – it's a sin not to do so." Elizabeth said to Sally.

"You right." Sally confirmed, "We just guardians 'cause all the riches really belong to God. We must share it with his people... We just the temporary caretakers. Some people, including our husbands, just don't understand it's God's will."

The two ladies began to make plans to have the roofs, on the share-cropper's shacks, repaired while they avoided the topic of how they came to be so well off. Elizabeth McDonald and Sally Ryan did not want to think about how their forefathers included their slaves on their list of properties along with their livestock. As ladies of society, they opted to ignore the shroud of unresolved conflict about slavery. If they didn't think about it, then the source of their family's wealth could not hamper their present day spiritual development; regardless of the fact that their family still benefited from that accumulated wealth every day... The wealth they ultimately inherited.

Both ladies had closets full of bounty from many shopping trips to New York, Atlanta, and even Paris: the fur coats, the fashionable suits by Channel, the Chantilly lace gowns, the Milan straw hats, the soft Egyptian cotton summer dresses, and the diamond rings and brooches; the cut crystal goblets, the Lenox china, the crystal chandeliers, the sterling silver tea sets, serving trays and flat-wear - stored in soft individual felt envelopes and polished every week by the household help, and the small but respectable art collection that hung on the walls - works of Picasso, Monet, and the famed abstract impressionist Jackson Pollock were some of the features of leisure and material goods that pleasured their families.

Their growing sense of complicity and concern, about the plight of poor people, was better for Elizabeth and Sally to digest while they continued to enjoy their affluent lifestyle if they considered their inherited wealth as a stroke of good luck, or as God's will. Certainly their parents had not done anything sinister to accumulate that wealth... Surely it was a blessing from God.

However, Elizabeth McDonald never forgot that the land, on Price Road, originally belonged to her family. She never actually mentioned that fact to her husband, but Elizabeth thought about it when he made her angry. Whatever money, or status in the community, Mr. Richard McDonald had was mostly because he married Elizabeth Ryan. As her husband, Dick received the benefit of his wife's inheritance. The same was true of Sally Ryan since she was married to Elizabeth's brother, Allen. Sally was always conscious of her position in the trail of family money. Her mother reiterated that fact to her all the time; therefore, Sally Ryan walked the fine line of cooperation, collaboration, support, or reinforcement, depending on the prevalent situation within the family affairs. Still, most situations placed Sally and Elizabeth on the same side - such was the case regarding the roofs for the sharecropper's houses.

"You a lucky girl Sally... Allen's a handsome man, and he's rich too. A man who is happy at home don't have no reason to stray..." Sally's mother always said. "You do whatever makes him happy... You be a good wife..."

Sally respected her mother's advice, and she did everything she could think of to be a good wife for Allen. She wore the clothes Allen laid out for her to wear every day, whether she liked his choice or not. He was meticulous in his own appearance; sometimes changing his clothes, from skin out, more than twice a day. It was important to Allen that his lightly starched shirts were color coordinated, and his cuff links and tie pins were always adjusted to create perfect geometric angles.

Sally soon discovered that her husband was uncompromising about the fashion choices he made for both her and their daughter. Sally re-signed herself to that fact, and she wore her hair in the styles Allen wanted; he bought all of her makeup, and sometimes even applied it for her. Sally had a drawer full of leather gloves: long ones, short ones, leather gloves of every color. Sally was not fond of leather gloves, but she wore them to make her husband happy.

It was Allen, who picked the white eyelet fabric and designed the bassinet cover to be made for their baby girl, and Sally didn't say a mumbling word – even though it was not something she would have chosen. And, Allen supervised the dressmaker when she measured the hem of Sally's skirts. "No shorter than 12" from the floor." he insisted. Allen always could comb and style their little girl's hair better than she could; consequently, Sally allowed him that job. And Sally was always conscious to give her husband compliments about anything he did in her effort to follow her mother's advice. Whenever Allen and his best friend, Gregory, went on weekend fishing trips, Sally breathed freely. And Allen was actually pleased when his wife shared so much time with his sister; that was the easy part because Sally Ryan really enjoyed Elizabeth's company. She admired Elizabeth's gumption…

Lora Berry actually liked working for Mrs. McDonald, she was a fair woman; Mr. McDonald, however, was another story. He gave her a clammy feeling; Lora tried to make sure she was never alone with him – which sometimes took real effort. Lora noticed that Mr. McDonald called all his sharecroppers **Niggra's**, even though some of them were 'White' people; in fact, she knew several of them. Clyde Parker and his family didn't live far from her. She wondered how Mr. Parker would feel if he knew the bank president labeled him as a 'Nigger'.

"Poor White people are the same as us, they just don't know it." Lora remarked to Oran, as they laid in their bed one night.

"Why you say so?" Oran asked.

"Cause the wealthier White folks call po' White folks 'Niggras' behind their backs". Lora replied.

"Po' White people, like Clyde Parker, think when they 'round other White folks they equal - 'cause they White too. Ain't true. They ain't equal." Lora continued.

"Rich White folks don't think po' White people, like Clyde Parker, are the same as other White people - 'cause they po'. But, those po' White people - they think they better than us 'cause they was born with white skin… But, it don't matter if they White; they still po', and rich White people call them Nigga's – 'cept the po' Whites don't know it." Lora said as she cuddled up to her husband.

Oran Berry wrapped his arms around his wife; it was about the same time that Elizabeth McDonald got on her knees to say her evening prayers.

"God please give me the wisdom and insight 'bout how ta use our money so dat me 'n Dick can get inta heav'n." Elizabeth prayed. Then, instead of getting into bed alone, Elizabeth settled into a comfortable position in the rocking chair by the window. The rocking motion of the chair was soothing. Elizabeth remembered sitting on her mother's lap in the same chair as a child. Elizabeth knew it would be late in the evening, if at all, when her husband came home. She waited every night…

As Elizabeth reached for her eyeglasses on the table, she remembered why her mother always sat in the rocking chair – the same rocking chair at the end of each day. Suddenly there was an understanding… It hit Elizabeth's brain like a sledgehammer. It dawned on Elizabeth that she was following a family ritual. Elizabeth spoke out to the empty chambers of her beautiful home.

"I'm different; I've got ma Bible… I don't need da 'hot toddies' like Ma had every night." she said as if to reassure herself of something. Then Elizabeth McDonald adjusted her glasses and began to read her Bible while she waited for her Richard to come home. She resented the temptation to make herself a nightcap, or to use that white powdered substance she bought on her last cruise. The small envelop hidden in her handkerchief drawer was almost empty; Elizabeth knew she had to be careful not to use the last of that feel-good-white-stuff because she didn't know when she would be able to replenish her supply. It always made her relax enough to fall asleep, yet she tried not to use it every night…

The old folks said… "*It is easier for a camel to go through the eye of a needle than for a rich man to enter the kingdom of God.*" Luke 18:25

The church ladies said… "*The Lord openeth the eyes of the blind.*" Psalm 146:8

BLOOD ON THE GROUND

The mailboxes for the families who lived in the two dilapidated farmhouses were placed where a wide dirt path hung off Price Road like the arm of a skeleton – the bare bones, the carcass remains of plantation life. The neighbors knew the path as Tobacco Road because of its purpose of existence. The two mailboxes were the only thing that called attention to Tobacco Road's link to Price Road; it was an unmarked appendage to the highway, and the only access route to the homes of the sharecroppers.

The deep furrows in the dirt, where tobacco sleds and wagons passed for so many years, had formed a hump in the middle of Tobacco Road. As if in fear of their own survival, a few brave blades of grass peeked through the hard clay on top of the mound that rose in the middle of the road. Thick foliage surrounded the worn, hardened, cracked, grooved, overworked earth on Tobacco Road as it ambled from the highway toward the shacks and the tobacco fields. About 500 feet from Price Road, an abundance of plant life forced a split in Tobacco Road as it proceeded in separate directions toward the homes of Oliver Shaw and Clyde Parker. The two farms were separated by the natural formation of a line of eight foot pine trees and the ethnicity of the poor sharecroppers who worked the land.

Ed drove past both mailboxes without stopping. He didn't have any mail to deliver to the Shaws nor the Parkers. Ed knew he was probably being watched from a distance even though he couldn't see anyone. The Shaw and Parker families worked hard as sharecroppers. The large fields of tobacco, all around Tobacco Road, were confirmation of how much effort the farmers put forth every day.

Both the Shaw and the Parker families were extremely poor, and they worked together to insure the yearly earnings from both farms were sufficient - as meager as the results may be. It was a smart business decision – a matter of basic survival - for all. Clyde Parker, Oliver Shaw, and their respective families, shared everything pertaining to

45

their farms: they worked together in each other's fields, sometimes they ate together, and they drank the clear cool well water from the same dipper; their children played together and exchanged their outgrown clothes and toys with each other - without any notice of skin color.

However, the close relationship of the families was never acknowledged when they were away from their farms. When the Parkers and the Shaws saw each other on Washington Street, in Leaksville, they barely spoke to each other. They did even not sit next to each other at the bus station, or on the bus, because the Parkers sat proudly in the seats marked for White folks at the front of the bus. In town the Shaw family drank water from a fountain under a '**Colored Only**' sign while the Parkers drank from the '**White Only**' water fountain. When he was around other White people, Mr. Parker carried himself in a prejudicial manner. At those times, Clyde Parker treated Oliver Shaw as if he were a piece of hot coal – an object that Clyde didn't want his hand to touch.

When Clyde was back on his farm, and there were no other White people around, he exhibited a totally different personality. It was as if the ego of the city-proud bigoted Clyde Parker was banished; whereas, the non-judgmental attitude of a more genteel Clyde Parker reappeared in the same body - back on the farm. Clyde Parker tried to explain his system of dealing with Colored people to his wife and children because he wanted them to understand how to act the same way.

"I know we needs Oliver an'em ta help us with our crops… We needs da help, but since we'ze White, we'ze better 'n dem - in God's sight. So we ac' like other White people when we'ze in town, so az other people of our kind knows we know our place. We know that we'ze s'pose to do dat - cause we is White. All White folks knows dat's a fact." Clyde said to his family.

Clyde Parker's hypocrisy annoyed Oliver Shaw beyond imagination. If Oliver could make his yearly harvest without Clyde Parker's help, he would not be so accepting of the two faces of Clyde Parker. Until he had that enlightening conversation with Lora Berry, Oliver harbored unfathomable scorn toward Clyde Parker - which he concealed behind pleasantries. Whereas, since his conversation with Lora,

Oliver Shaw actually felt a level of sympathy for Clyde and the other White folk like him who thought in such a bigoted manner.

"Po' white folks are pitiful; they have a need to feel superior over something... That's hard ta do when dey so poor dey can't even feed dar own children." said Oliver Shaw to his family after a trip into town.

Oliver's youngest child did not understand why he couldn't sit at the front of the bus next to his white playmate, Mr. Parker's little son. Oliver tried to explain to his children that White people, including the Parkers, have an emotional need to be treated as if they were the race that God chose to rule the universe. Oliver Shaw was convinced that if the majority of White people (rich or poor) were not able to attain, and maintain, their perceived feeling of superiority over people of color (black, brown, or yellow) they became psychotic.

"Of course dat's not how all White folks feel; it seems ta only apply to 'dose White people who really don't feel good 'bout 'demselves." Oliver said.

"But Poppa, why ya say White folks don't feel good about 'demselves if they think 'dey better than everybody?" Oliver's little son asked.

"Well, it's sort'a hard to 'xplain" Oliver said.

"It's like'a bully in school dat tries to scare 'erybody 'cause he's 'fraid somebody will find out how stupid 'n dumb he really is. Fo' da bully ta be in control, he acts mean... Makes 'erybody do what he says; den, nobody'll find out how scared da bully really is 'n what he don't know." Oliver continued...

"So da White folk who act like'a mean bully are really scared. Fact is... da more control a person has to have – da more insecure he really is." Oliver said.

Oliver had many examples to support his reasoning. He had stored the memories of his past in the recesses of his mind. Oliver's past only came forward when an unwelcome breeze entered the cavity of his brain where the memories were stored. This time the bus incident was the breeze that came through to allow him to share vital information about his past with his children - which they needed to know; therefore, Oliver proceeded to tell his children about some experiences in his life - experiences he wished he could forget... Oliver knew that the day would come when he would have to speak his memories aloud… The day had arrived. With effort, he found his voice…

"My father t'was lynched by'a mob of rednecks." Oliver words were soft, but his statement was heavy.

Oliver started his recall gradually… He had the full attention of all his children, and he did not try to hide the deep surge of emotion that engulfed him.

"Dey were all po' White folks… De mob was led by a po' White man who t'was mad with ma father 'cause my father didn't call him '**Mr.**' when there were other White people 'round." Oliver said.

"Understand what I'm saying… Ma father had da audacity to call a White man - dat he knew all his life, by his first name in front of other White people." Oliver spoke slowly, with controlled anger. He only said a few words, yet Oliver sighed; tiredness came over him. His shoulders sloped under the pressure of the weight of the words he had yet to speak.

"And, for that he died!" Oliver continued.

"I can't forget what happened dat day. It'll never leave ma mind's eye." Oliver shook his head as if it were possible to shake the memory out of his head.

"I was just'a little boy when it happened; such horrible things should never have ta be experienced by anyone, 'specially little children." Oliver paused for a moment… He took a little time to compose himself before he continued.

"The mob rode onto our farm - shooting rifles and yelling fo my mother ta come outside. Momma hid behind da door, all us children - we was behind her… holding onto her fo' dear life. A body was thrown out on da dirt yard, and da mob rode off - laughing. After dey left, Momma opened da door. Daddy was lying dead on da ground, with da thick rope still 'round his neck…" Oliver stopped for a moment seemingly to catch the breath that was hard for his chest to expel; this was the first time he told his children this memory. It was hard!

"I was seven years old… Ma mom let out a blood curdling scream dat I will never forget; she collapsed on da ground. I had ta help Momma pull ma dead Daddy into the house. Da blood ran out'a Daddy's mouth – on'ta de ground. Da blood made a line where we pulled him. Daddy was too big and heavy for us ta pick up ta carry, and it t'was real hard ta pull 'm." Oliver continued while his children sat in wide-eyed silence.

"I tried ta sweep da blood away, even covered it with da yard dirt, but it kept coming back. My daddy's blood refused ta'be hidden; it just kept reappearing, like he's not going ta let people forget he died on dis land – that he shed his blood on dis land. If I go back to dat house right now I can show you dat line of blood on da ground. It's still there… It's never going away. My daddy's blood is part of this earth; in fact, I'll do that… I'll take you ta see your grandfather's blood on da ground… Maybe you'll understand better what I'm saying." Oliver paused to mull over the idea of taking his children to see his father's blood. He felt that the sight of the everlasting blood of their grandfather, their ancestor, on that ground would help his children understand the power of the blood.

"We were taught, as Christians, ta believe that Jesus' blood was da sacrifice paid fo' all our sins; well, I believe dat my father's blood t'was da sacrifice he paid fo' da price of freedom fo' all of his descendants… Dat's all of us." Oliver told his children.

"I believe da same is true fo' all da children of all of de Black people whose blood has been shed on this ground." he continued.

"As their children, we do hav'a responsibility. We must become da best people we came be. Da freedom our ancestors worked and died fo' can never be ours if we remain ignorant… It's da job of da generations, following da genocide, ta get a good education. Freedom ain't nothing if you don't know how ta use it." Oliver explained.

"You ma father's heirs, you don't have ta mix your own blood with his in dis dirt. Your generation don't have ta do da dying, da blood of all da black mothers 'n fathers should be 'nough ta pay de price for our freedom; no matter what de cost - de price is already paid!" Oliver said.

Oliver's lack of a formal education did not show as he spoke his wisdom to his children. It was as if he was the designated spokesperson for all of his forefathers. Oliver was self taught; he spent many nights reading by kerosene lamp or candle light. Even though Oliver

Shaw was a sharecropper, he was well-read. He did not just pick his thoughts from the air; Oliver was a man who researched; his thoughts and conclusions were grounded, and his theories could be supported by documentation. Next to his farming tools, Oliver Shaw's books were his most valuable possessions.

Oliver continued to teach his children… Was it his imagination, or did Oliver really feel something grip his shoulder? It felt like his father's hand… When Oliver was a little boy his father always walked with his hand on his shoulder. Oliver quickly glanced back over his shoulder; he almost expected to see a tall muscular figure there. Oliver Shaw always felt a spiritual connection with his murdered father… He always found strength in his father's invincible blood. Oliver realized as he spoke to his children that the intergenerational spiritual connection he constantly felt with his father was suddenly more intense than ever before.

"God didn't make no mistakes, 'n he loves ya just like ya are." Oliver assured his children.

"Ya don't have ta be mean ta people in order for you ta prove you're better den anyone else – ya'r feeling like that don't make God love you no more… You know y'all smart; y'all beautiful, God gave you that… And, you won't be poor always. You'll get your own money when ya get ya'r own education… God got gifts for ya that ya can't even see yet. You get yourself prepared ta receive God's gifts; he can't give them ta you 'til you ready ta handle his goodness." Oliver said.

"You got'ta be smart - work hard for your dreams, 'n God'll help ya… You don't need to care 'bout what someone say; ya know truth for yo'self. And, as part of ya education, ya must b'come more knowledge-able 'bout White folks than dey are 'bout themselves. As Black people we have ta understand our adversaries, so'as our people don't get caught unawares and end up in slavery again." Oliver lectured to his children.

"You got proof dat God loves you… Do ya realize that African people are de only ones dat God made with hair dat stands straight up? That's 'cause it reaches naturally toward heaven. It's like we 'specially close to God 'cause we in a constant state of worship and praise. Not just on Sundays, and not just at church. God likes praise – praise is different from a prayer you know. God made our hair stand up, so we can be naturally praising him all da time. So, what we need ta worry 'bout what some White people thinking bout us for? We got God... God knows our tribulations, and he gives us de strength 'n wisdom ta bear our troubles." Oliver said.

It was important to Oliver that his children had a feeling of self worth! Oliver knew, in his soul, that a good education and self respect were the main survival keys. Oliver Shaw didn't have much schooling, but he was determined to make sure his children became college graduates; their lives were not going to be as hard as his.

Oliver Shaw felt compelled, with every fiber in his being, to do everything he could to make sure his children understood how they must behave in the presence of all White folks; moreover, why those actions were necessary. His children must live every day as if they were passing through a dangerous jungle, and as their father, Oliver was their guide. Oliver knew if he failed to make his children understand how to avoid the traps of racial quicksand, and to control the wild animals in that jungle; he couldn't bear the possible consequences.

Some people interpreted Oliver's teachings to his children as 'Uncle Tomish'; in fact, his wife felt that way in the beginning. But, Mrs. Oliver Shaw soon understood that her husband was conveying a survival technique; she began to accept Oliver's philosophy. Mrs. Shaw agreed with her husband, they must teach their children tactics necessary to exist in a dangerous environment. As Black children, their lives depended upon their comprehension, and quick perception, of any given situation. Oliver wanted his children to realize that, even when laws were changed, people's souls didn't automatically change. Oliver's father was one of the hundreds of Black people who were killed after the Emancipation Proclamation – just because they were born black... The existing new law didn't matter. Oliver intended to make sure, even though he was only a poor sharecropper - and not formally educated, that his children acquired the mental strength and self confidence necessary to withstand the world they faced. They needed to know when, how, and where to fight the freedom fight – intelligently.

The church ladies said…"*The Lord don't put on you any more that you can bear.*"

The old folks said… *"If we could sell our experiences for what they cost us, we'd have so much money we'd never have to work again."*

The church ladies said… *"The secret things belong unto the Lord our God: but those things which are revealed belong unto us and to our children forever, that we may follow all the words of this law."* Deuteronomy 30:29

BIG MOM

Further down the road Ed approached three mailboxes. The first mailbox, marked for Illanna and Perry Wheatley, had not been used for two years; the house it represented was about fifty yards away. Ed's eyes darted in that direction; a lump lodged unexpectedly in his throat at the sight of the high weeds and squirrels that now made the Wheatley house their home. It still seemed strange to him that Illanna and Perry Wheatley were no longer there; the thought of them brought a warm feeling to Ed's heart. He missed seeing Illanna when she worked around her house with Perry, her devoted husband and helpmate, always by her side. Illanna died one day, and Perry couldn't seem to live without her. Perry died, it seemed of a broken heart, before Illanna's funeral could be planned; therefore, the family delayed her burial in order to hold the funeral for both of them.

Ed smiled as he remembered the couple; his mind always went to the image of Jack Sprat and his wife whenever he saw them. Perry was over 6' tall and lean while Illanna', who was pleasantly plump, was only about 5 foot 2 inches tall; still, everyone lovingly called her 'Big Mom.' Illanna's cinnamon skin was sprinkled with dark brown age moles. The moles just kept appearing all over Illanna's body, without warning; the same thing happened to her mother as she aged, that was why Illanna called them age moles.

Illanna always wore her hair in the exact same style. Everyday Illanna pulled her hair tight, twisted it into a large bun at the center top of her head, and secured it in place with the four large black Onyx hairpins which once belonged to her mother; in fact, it was the exact hairstyle her mother wore. Illanna's mother died shortly after Illanna married Perry; the hairpins were Illanna's wedding gift from her mother.

When she was a little girl, Illanna loved to watch her mom place the beautiful Onyx hairpins in her hair while she sat in front of a delicate glass dressing table. Illanna thought her mother's rectangle shaped glass tray, with the inset mirror, that sat atop the glass dressing table

53

was the most beautiful thing she had ever seen. The tray had a gold plated design of swirls and scallops that danced around its edge. Illanna's mother had a grooming set (hairbrush, comb, and hand mirror), which matched the gold plated design on the glass tray; she always placed each item, in the middle of the tray, upside down, and in a neat row. Illanna still had the glass tray and the Onyx hairpins, so every morning when Illanna placed the hairpins in her hair the memories of her mother were vivid in her mind's eye. That was all she had, other than one photograph, to remind her of her mother.

"Honey, I'm praying dat Perry will be a good husband." Illanna's mother said when she handed her newly wed daughter the only gift she could afford.

"I was told that da Onyx originated from de body of Venus. As da story goes, mischievous Cupid cut Venus's fingernails while she was 'sleep - her nail clippings became da Onyx. Da rich black color t'was supposed ta represent regeneration and a new beginning. The wearer of de Onyx stone would have de gift of eloquence, true love, 'n romance in life. I wish for you dat your true love stay true forever." Illanna's mother told her.

"My mother t'was right; d'ese hairpins are what keeps us together." Illanna jokily said to Perry.

Perry was the regressive, silent type; he was very supportive - always in the background - ready to do whatever Big Mom needed. Illanna loved Perry deeply; she did not wait for special moments to say, "I love you Perry Wheatley." Sometimes they shared an affectionate moment, with a twinkle of their eyes silently connecting over the heads of their grandchildren as they all worked in the garden, side by side; those moments usually went unnoticed by the family. And, the family never observed how Perry watched, adoringly, as Illanna took the Onyx pins out of her hair every night. He always found joy when Illanna released her long locks to fall, without restraint, around her shoulders.

Perry and Illanna's house was always full of activity; it was a gathering place for all their children, grandchildren, nieces, nephews, sisters, and brothers. At some point in their lives, an assortment of their extended family lived with Illanna and Perry. Big Mom was willing to do everything she could to help her family get ahead in life. No one was surprised when Illanna and Perry, accepted the responsibility for the care of most of their grandchildren while five of their own six children moved away from home - at various times throughout the years. Most of the Wheatley children followed each other to Baltimore, Maryland; each move left more grandchildren at Big Mom's house.

"Big Mom, I'll be back ta get my children as soon as possible… As soon as I get myself together." said every Wheatley offspring as they left home with their parents' blessings.

Whenever Ed passed Big Mom's house, he still couldn't resist the instinct to look to see if Illanna was working in her yard, even though he knew darn well no-one was there. Ed remembered how religiously Illanna followed a self imposed weekly routine. Every Monday she always had three large tin tubs set up in the yard, full of water, for the laundry. She could be seen leaning over the scrub board pumping both arms up and down until the chosen garment was cleaned to her satisfaction. The two other tubs, in turn, held the rinse water. Tuesday was the day to iron, Wednesday was the day to sew, and on Thursday Illanna washed and waxed the linoleum floors throughout her house. Ed would always see Illanna with Perry and some of the children-in-resident nearby as she: worked in her vegetable or flower gardens, drew water from the well, chopped wood for the stove, or swept the dirt yard. Sometimes she was on the front porch - plaiting a child's hair, and handing the child the loose hair that was trapped in the teeth of the comb.

"Here child - hold dis hair tight in yo'r hand, don't let it get 'way from ya! When I finish ya take dat hair 'n burn it." Illanna told whoever she was grooming…

"If ya don't burn de hair a bird might use it fo' its nest. If a bird makes a nest out'ta ya hair, ya'll hav'a migraine headache for da rest of ya life. Ya don't want dat do ya? No - don't waste no time child, burn dat ball of hair!" Illanna mandated.

Illanna always had something to do; even when she was supposed to be relaxing Illanna was busy doing something. If she was sitting in the rocking chair there was a crochet or knitting needle in her hand…

Always busy… Energy seemed to explode out of Illanna… Ed missed that energy… He missed Illanna.

Most of the houses along the highway had electricity; however, there were still a few homes in the vicinity of Price Road that still did not have electricity. Some families, whose homes had electricity, may not have had many of the modern appliances - just the lights. Illanna' home was one of those. She had a ceiling light in each room, a lonely bare bulb that hug at the end of a long black cord. Illanna and Perry saved money for months to buy an electric stove. One year the adults in the family bought a Frigidaire from Sears instead of Christmas gifts.

At first the Wheatley grandchildren were upset, but they got over it. They all enjoyed the tangerines that Big Mom managed to give them. Tangerines were special treats which the Wheatleys could only afford once a year. Besides, the children liked to stand in the doorway of the new Frigidaire and feel the cold air it emitted on hot days. Illanna's grandchildren knew better than to let Big Mom catch them with the refrigerator door open, so one child would be the lookout while they took turns cooling off.

A tired Illanna sat on her porch at the end of each day while she yelled instructions to the children – directions for them to get ready for bed:

"Get yo nightgown on… Wash up now - make de sign of de cross, ya'll know what I mean – ya face, under ya arms and between yo legs. And don't forget to use soap… Stop that running 'round! Don't ya spill that water! Be careful! I'm going ta give ya'll a whipping if ya don't behave yar'self… Gal, bring me a comb so I can do ya hair… Leave h'm alone… Stop running…" Big mom's voice was loud, commanding, and yet gently gruff.

Most of the houses along Price Road did not have running water, or indoor toilets, until the 1950s. Like most of the families during those days, Big Mom placed a large tin tub in the middle of the kitchen on bath days. The bath water was heated in iron kettles on the wood stove; the precut wood for the stove was cut daily and stored underneath a tarp in the backyard.

Big Mom warned the children to be careful and watch for snakes when they got firewood. Once, when Illanna was a child, she almost touched a rattlesnake that was curled up in a wood pile; she never forgot it… Everyone told her that the snake must have been ready to strike because it was in a curled position and made its tail rattle - which was the only reason Illanna even noticed the rattlesnake in the first place. Big Mom's fear of snakes was deep-seated; it was in every fiber of her existence.

"Watch out child… Look good before you touch anything… Always look down at the ground… Watch where you walking!" Big Mom always warned the children.

Saturday night was bath night; the social atmosphere of the kitchen changed to become a private place for an individual to bathe - everybody took turns. It was a job, all by itself, to keep the mischievous children away from the kitchen when another child was trying to take a private Saturday night bath. The children loved to tease and annoy the bather; they created more havoc than Big Mom was able to endure at her age. Because of the chaos, Big Mom half-heartedly monitored the children's bedtime progression from her favorite rocking chair while her knitting needles clicked in syncopation as she worked on something… Big Mom was always working on something… Always working…

It had been two years since anyone lived in the Wheatley house, but no-one wanted to remove the mailbox. Ed stopped to place mail into the second mailbox in the group of three. Next to the unused Wheatley mailbox stood the mailbox that belonged to Iris and Natan Ross.

Iris, the oldest Wheatley child, was the only offspring who didn't move to Baltimore. Iris lived in the newer ranch style house on the lot next to her parents' home - with her husband, Natan Ross, and his two children from his previous marriage; in addition, Iris's fragile young cousin, Jazmaine Sage, and Jazmaine's baby boy, Jarrah, have lived with Iris since Perry and Illanna's deaths when they became Iris's responsibility. Although she never experienced childbirth, Iris was a mother to four children.

Illanna and Iris went to visit their family in Baltimore, Maryland only once. It was the first time either Illanna or Iris had ever been out of North Carolina; in fact, it was the first time they had been more than thirty miles from Price Road in their entire lives. Perry and Natan,

Iris's husband, didn't go; they stayed at home to keep the farms, the men had little time for vacations.

Weldon, Illanna's oldest son, drove down from Baltimore one summer weekend in his classy new Black 1949 Ford to take his mother and sister for the visit. He was so proud of the sleek, revolutionary car with the trademark circle on the shinny chrome grille. It was the first car anyone in the family ever owned. Weldon returned to Baltimore with his mother and sister riding on the plush leather seats. Neither Illanna nor Iris had ever ridden in such a nice car; furthermore, they had never seen a city as enormous as Baltimore. Their questions were endless...

"Why da houses so close ta'gether?" Iris asked in amazement. "Makes me feel claustrophobic, need me some air space ta breath, how y'all do it?" Big Mom said as she fanned her hand in the air - pretending she was smothering.

"Dey called row houses Big Mom; you'll get use ta it."

"Why every house look just like the other one? How you tell which one is y'all's?" Iris asked her brother.

"All the houses have numbers on dem like dat - 906, 908, 910... See... De even numbers all on one side of da street; de odd numbers on da other side." Weldon replied.

"I don't see no mailboxes... Where is y'all's mailboxes?" Illanna wondered.

"Theys in da front door, see that slot at de bottom of da door? That's da mailbox; de mail just fall inside de house. Some houses have'a long narrow box hug on de door frame; mailman puts da mail in dhere." Illanna's son explained patiently.

"All de houses got those white steps, is dey real marble? How y'all keep dem so clean?" The questions and comments continued as consistent as string beans being snapped on Illanna's front porch - from both Illanna and Iris.

"Too much cement fo' me, I need me some'a God's dirt under ma feet."

"Don't dat cement make it real hot in da summer?"

"How y'all keep cool?"

"What is dat thing? Look like'a bus, but ain't got no wheels?"

"Big Mom, that's called a trolley, it runs on tracks, runs on electricity from dose wires running overhead. I'll take you for a ride while yo'all here." Illanna's son answered, as he was to retell the story later, with the patience of Job.

"Don't know if ya will or not, don't know if I want'a be in no box with 'lectricity running through it!" Big Mom said laughing - pretending to be afraid.

"Dis car has 'lectricity in it Big Mom."

"What! Why didn't you tell me dat before? Maybe I wouldn't ha' come on dis here trip!" said Illanna as she pretended to be overly surprised... Actually she was intrigued; electricity was new to Illanna, and it still mesmerized her. She was glad to have lived long enough to be able to use its technology. Illanna was not really afraid of electricity and its many uses, but she was definitely in awe of it.

Illanna was enjoying her trip, but she had already decided that she did not want to spend too much time in Baltimore... She allowed her children to laugh at her decision to go back home early - aborting her vacation.

"Big Mom was 'fraid of the trolleys. She called da trolleys rolling electric rectangles without tires, so she wanted to go home." Illanna's children later told their citified Baltimore friends.

Illanna never said a mumbling word; she allowed her children to presume it was the fear of new things which made her want to return so quickly to North Carolina. But, that wasn't it at all. Yes - Illanna did have a fear; however, she feared something entirely different. It was the fear of loosing her grandchildren to the narrow, tight, irreverent streets of Baltimore, Maryland - with the rows of white marble steps and close houses. No indeed, her grandchildren were better off on Price Road where there was enough space for children and flowers to grow... So, Illanna and Iris asked Weldon to drive them back to their homes, their sanctuary, and neither would ever leave Price Road again.

* * *

Natan Ross, who was almost twenty years older than his wife, Iris, was a successful tobacco farmer. He owned about twenty acres of the farmland that extended along Price Road, beginning with the property next to the Wheatley house. Natan Ross was a widower who was left with two children when his wife died of pneumonia while their youngest child was still a baby. Natan passionately set his eyes on his seventeen year old neighbor, a very young blossoming Iris, shortly after his wife died. Natan did not try to hide his lust for Iris, nor his need for a caregiver for his children; therefore, no-one was surprised when Natan asked Iris to marry him, and she accepted.

There was no bona fide courtship; it was not a passionate hot blooded love that Iris felt, but she could endure a marriage with the promise of tenderness and devotion. Iris felt the wifely duties were little to exchange for the assurance of financial security - in addition to being able to live so close to her mother. Natan understood and respected Iris' feelings. It didn't matter. It was easy for him to love her; she was a young, beautiful, and sweet woman. Natan vowed to be the best husband in the world, and he worked at that promise everyday. The commodity type arraignment worked for both. Natan Ross needed a mother for his children, and a wife for his manly needs; Iris Wheatley needed security. Iris never felt that she made a wrong decision; she respected Natan, even if she didn't feel the passion of romantic love.

The old folks said… *"You don't miss what you never had."*

Iris Wheatley Ross and Rozlyn Berry grew up as close friends and neighbors. As teenagers they often shared their feelings with each other about the future they anticipated; moreover, they overheard the church ladies talk about how all girls needed to get married before they got 'too' old.

"Why do people throw rice on the couple after the wedding?" One asked the Other.

"I don't know, maybe the rice falling is symbolic of a storm. Maybe people think if it rains rice after the wedding ceremony the only storms the couple will have to face will at least give them something to eat." The Other answered with a laugh.

"Well, I don't think it works." commented One; then, the One and the Other laughed together. Iris and Rozlyn noticed that within a few months after the wedding the brides, who ran under the rain storm of rice, began to express disappointment with their married life. The newlywed's conversations sounded like a requiem for an exciting love, one that sadly died a slow and painful death - like notes of sad music. At any rate, some of the young new wives began to show: burrows across their foreheads, deep creases around their mouths, and dark puffiness around their eyes... Rozlyn noticed something else... Whenever a group of married women got together, their conversation always seemed to resort to the pain and length of childbirth.

"Is that all married women have to talk about?" Rozlyn questioned. "And, it seems, to me, that married life is making the women look older while they are still so young." she told Iris.

"That's the look of maturity." The church ladies insisted.

"I don't want to be that mature!" Rozlyn whispered to Iris. Rozlyn was still a teenager, but she already knew what she *didn't* want her life to become.

Iris thought about that conversation after she had been married for several years. Iris believed she had made the right decision; she had done exactly what she told Rozlyn she was going to do when they were fourteen years old and discussed their future.

"When I marry it'll be ta a man who loves me more than I love him, and he'll be financially stable. I want a comfortable life - don't have ta be rich, just comfortable; den, I'll be content." Iris told Rozlyn.

Years later, Iris was still satisfied with her life as Mrs. Natan Ross - not a giddy happy, but satisfied... Iris was thankful that she never felt that sense of frustration she and Rozlyn saw in so many other wives. She never had exotic expectations concerning her marriage; therefore, Iris was content. She and Rozlyn still kept in touch; their friendship remained intact throughout the years although Rozlyn no longer lived on Price Road. Iris sometimes thought about the time Rozlyn said to her, "Only cows are content." It was a comment from a Pet Milk advertisement; nevertheless it made Iris pause to think... Yet, Iris concluded -'*content*' was still the only word that described how she felt in her marriage.

Iris thought to herself as she prepared for bed... Big Mom had more than contentment in her marriage... Iris fondled the Onyx hairpins she had worn in her hair for two years as she placed them on the glass tray. Iris tried not to wake up Natan when she laid down in the bed next to him. She wondered… Did the Onyx hairpins really bring her parents a blessed marriage? Maybe so… At least she knew it wasn't the rice.

The old folks said… *"Eagles fly alone; they do not have to fly with a flock."*

The church ladies said… *"Wives submit yourself unto your own husbands as to the Lord."* Ephesians 5:22

Begonia Willow

The third mailbox in the cluster belonged to Sylvester and Begonia Willow. Ed O'Reilly knew more than any one person about all the families on Price Road. He knew: when they expected mail, when they received their mail, when they had problems, and how they solved their problems. Ed was like a gourmet spice in a pot of stew; it influenced the flavor without being seen, yet if it was not there, everyone could tell the difference. Ed O'Reilly loved to be in the mix; therefore, he was hardly ever absent from his job.

However, Ed was on a short sick leave when Illanna's nephew, Sylvester Willow, moved to Price Road. When Ed returned to work, Sylvester and his bride, Begonia, had already moved into the vacant old house across the road diagonally from Illanna's house; the Willow's presence completed the mailbox trio alongside those of the Wheatly's and the Ross'.

Sylvester Willow was the son of Illanna Wheatly's oldest sister. Sylvester fell madly in love with his high school sweetheart, Begonia. Their youthful love was fresh, pure, and impatient; so much so, that they married impulsively - based on the emotions of the heart rather than a plan. After their impromptu wedding, they didn't have a place to live; therefore, the young couple began married life living with Sylvester's mother - whose house was already overcrowded. Illanna, who was aware of the situation, told Sylvester about the empty house for rent on Price Road.

"The house needs some repairs," Illanna told him, "but it has possibilities."

The young couple moved in. And, Begonia, Sylvester's enthusiastic wife, began to convert the old house into a stylish home. Begonia and Sylvester worked hard; they replaced windows, scrubbed, cleaned, and polished floors. Sylvester began to work for his Cousin Iris' husband, Natan Ross, in the tobacco fields. Meanwhile, Begonia made color co-ordinated curtains, throw pillows, bedspreads, dollies, and tablecloths.

Begonia patched, painted, and made floral murals on the walls; she even took the time to paint sunflowers and leaves on their mailbox. It was the most original mailbox on Price Road. To Illanna's delight the place across the road went from what looked like a pig sty to a magnificent flower garden.

The old folks said, "*The place one lives conveys so much about the people therein.*"

Begonia was a talented seamstress. She worked on an old Singer treadle sewing machine, with the black metal head trimmed in gold (a hand-me-down from her mother). Soon Begonia began to provide extra income to supplement whatever Sylvester made as a farm hand.

One day Oran Berry brought Begonia a large bag of discarded scraps of cotton fabric – end cuts from sheets and pillowcases he got from his job at Fieldcrest Mills. Oran noticed the bags of scraps in the trash bin in the back of the factory, and he asked his boss if he could have them.

"Don't care, ain't nothing but trash, you can take all you want." his boss told Oran.

Oran retrieved two to three large bags of scraps every week. The salvaged bags contained various lengths of 12" wide strips of 100% cotton fabric. There was an assortment of pastel colored prints, and coordinated solids; in addition, coordinated pieces of corded bias strips and lace were sometimes mixed in with the fabric. Oran divided the bags of scrap among several of the ladies along Price Road. He gave some of the fabric to his wife, Lora; then, he shared more with Freesia's Holly, who used them for her arts and crafts hobby, and Begonia Willow.

Begonia Willow appreciated the bags of scraps the most. The scraps were like a gold mine to Begonia, she converted them into unbelievable treasures - fancy, or not so fancy, and just plain cute children's outfits for all ages: dresses, blouses, jumpers, rompers, shirts, knickers, jackets, and pajamas. She combined crochet, smocking, and embroidery into one-of-a-kind designs; it was impossible to tell they were made from small scraps. Begonia began to acquire a reputation as a specialty designer of children clothes.

The church ladies allowed Begonia to hold a yard sale after church one Sunday, a few weeks before school started; for that opportunity she promised to make a 10% donation of her sales to the church's building fund - through the Willing Workers Club. It turned out to be a worthwhile fundraising project for the church ladies.

Begonia took the remaining garments, left-over from the church yard sale, to a clothing store in Greensboro. The owner of the store bought them without hesitation. Begonia let the product speak for itself; soon customers began to request the custom children's wear.

"Mrs. Willow, I'd like for my store to be your exclusive distributor in Greensboro. I like your line of children's wear, and I'd like to start with an order of a dozen pieces a week. Of course, we can increase our orders as time goes on if we can be the only ones in town to carry your line." the store owner said to an astonished Begonia.

"Of course," Begonia replied. "I'll bring you some papers to sign to that effect next week," as she tried to appear all professional like - cool, calm, and collected... Actually inside, undetected, Begonia's stomach quivered with delight.

Begonia was so excited she could hardly wait to tell Sylvester. Begonia didn't know much about business, but she had a talent and good sense. She went to the high school principal, Professor Wright, for advice; he helped her compose a contract format, order forms, and receipts... Begonia found herself in business... She sewed as fast as she could.

It was a challenge for Begonia to travel to Greensboro on the bus every week, but it is worth the ride. She chose to market her merchandise at a distance from Leaksville because she was conscious of her source of fabric, and she didn't want to come in contact with someone who might recognize the material - someone who might try to stop Oran's access to the scraps. While she rode in the back of the bus, with her suitcase full of children's clothes, Begonia made plans to take her creations to another store in Reidsville, a town which was about twenty-five miles from Greensboro. Sometimes she couldn't sleep at night because she couldn't shut her brain up... Begonia Willow thought of so many things to do, and she wanted to do it all.

It didn't take long for Begonia to become a major children's clothing supplier for stores in both Reidsville and Greensboro. Oran continued to bring her the bags of scraps, and Begonia ordered additional fabric from the Sears catalog. Soon she began to go on shopping trips to the fabric district in New York where the choices of unique fabrics were more plentiful. The Eight Avenue wholesale brokers would not allow Begonia to purchase from them, so she had to pay retail prices for her fabric; nevertheless, the trip was worth it because of the exclusive choices that could only be found in New York.

One day Begonia placed an envelope in her mailbox, which contained an order to Sears for more fabric. Suddenly, an idea popped onto Begonia's head - an obvious derivative of her action of preparing the mail order. She was so excited she couldn't wait for Sylvester to come home for lunch, so Begonia ran all the way out to the tobacco field to tell him about her idea.

"Sylvester, I think I can do a mail order business. I can make custom memory quilts through mail orders… What da you think?" She gasped breathlessly.

"What is a Memory Quilt?" Sylvester asked in bewilderment. He liked the fact that Begonia found something she loved to do, and the extra money certainly helped. They were beginning to have a little nest egg in savings. Begonia had an electric motor installed onto her treadle sewing machine, and she bought an old industrial Singer machine from a factory that went out of business.

Sylvester admitted that sometimes Begonia's ideas danced all around outside his head; he couldn't always keep up with her thinking. Sylvester hugged and kissed his wife as he swung her around in his strong arms; her feet kicked the air as if they were independent lunatics. Sylvester asked again, over Begonia's delighted laughter, "What in the world is a Memory Quilt?"

"Just what the name implies," she said. "It's a quilt that has pieces of fabric that make you remember good times in your life - like a usable album of memories." Begonia answered while she jumped away from Sylvester's long tickling arms.

Begonia ran an advertisement, for the Memory Quilt, in the Colored section of the local papers; it was the beginning of a mail order business. Begonia sent information kits, with pictures, to all the churches in the phone book. She offered an organized procedure for church clubs to take quilt orders as an innovative way to make money towards their own fundraising efforts; she passed out flyers everywhere...

The flyers were not fancy, the information was basic; finally, it was the word of mouth - the praise from satisfied customers that turned Begonia's fabric pieces into financial profit. Oran continued to keep an eye out for discarded scraps. Because of his contribution to her business, Begonia often made Oran's children some clothes; he didn't charge her for the bags of scraps, and she didn't consider herself paying him, it just fulfilled a need to show her appreciation in some way.

The old folks said... *"Some people's trash is another person's treasure."*

The church ladies said... *"Whenever you help others, it is inevitable that you will help yourself."*

Begonia and Iris talked and interacted as if they were sisters; the fact that Begonia was an in-law had been long forgotten. The two women continued to work together on many projects: quilting, canning, and making lunch for the farm hands. They took turns making sure that their uncle, J.K. - who lived nearby, had something to eat everyday. Meanwhile, the church ladies were watching the calendar. They couldn't wait to ask Begonia when she was going to have a baby.

The church ladies said... *The Lord wants you to be fruitful and multiply.*

THINGS ARE LIKE THEY ARE

Illanna's youngest brother, J.K. Sage, reappeared in town in 1955 for her funeral. The J.K Sage who returned home, to Price Road, was a shell of a man; he did not resemble the big, strong, robust, soldier who went away as a young man in 1940. When Perry died, Iris allowed her uncle J.K. to stay with her for a few days. Because Iris's house was already overcrowded, the family rallied together to help the destitute J.K buy a small piece of land from Iris' husband (Natan practically gave it to him). They put a small, one unit trailer on it; then, J.K was able to move just down the road from his family.

J.K. spent his days laying on the old rusty metal glider swing in front of the trailer. His arm hung off the seat and dangled limp toward the ground; his eye lids, at half mast, made it hard to determine whether he was asleep or awake. Empty wine and corn liquor bottles accumulated daily in a basket. He took the empty bottles to Black Bottom once a week to be refilled. J.K. never invited anyone into his home, that way he didn't have to give excuses for: the build up of trash, the pile of unwashed dishes, the unmade bed, the total disarray. Ed always waved at J.K. when he drove by the trailer; he hardly ever had any mail for J.K.

The first thing J.K did after he was drafted into the United States Army was to ask his childhood sweetheart to marry him. They married in 1940, shortly before J.K. left for boot camp. A little baby girl, Jazmine Sage, was born in 1941 while J.K was stationed in Europe. Ed never actually met J.K. until he returned home for Illanna's funeral, but even before then Ed felt a personal connection to J.K.

Ed's driving style changed as if by instinct. He began to drive slower, more cautious, as he neared the spot. He recalled the deadly car accident that killed J.K.'s wife. It happened just down the road apiece. Ed grasped the steering wheel tighter as he approached the site of the accident. He could not loose the image of the terrible accident he witnessed years ago... He could still see it...

A large white delivery truck came down Price Road – fast - just as a car turned onto Shady Grove Road; the truck couldn't stop fast enough, and the car was pushed into a tree on the church grounds. The car was crushed like an accordion.

Although Ed had only been on the job for a few months when the car accident happened, he was already friendly with the people on his route; therefore, he knew who was in the mangled car. Every cell in Ed's entire body recalled the same pain, anxiety, fear, and sorrow that he felt that on that dreadful day. It was hard for Ed to look at that tree – it still smacked of tragedy, yet he couldn't stop himself from looking every time he drove by. Someone planted a beautiful white rose bush at the base of the tree where the crushed car had been; the magnificent flowers shared the space with the large roots of the elderly tree and defiantly reappeared every year... Larger.

The accident occurred on a Wednesday afternoon; Ed was driving back down Price Road, on his return trip to the post office. It was Ed who instinctively drove as fast as he could to tell Big Mom what happened. He took Big Mom and Perry to the scene; they never stopped thanking him for that even though Ed told them that he didn't think he had done anything extraordinary. Ed remembered how he instinctively removed the mailbag from the passenger seat to let Big Mom sit in the front of the car because it was the right thing to do. Still, Ed remembered the sense of relief he felt when he saw that there were no other White people around; thank God, he didn't have to explain his actions to anyone.

As Ed looked back on that day, he wondered why such thoughts even entered his mind. As he relived his thinking at the time, Ed recalled the feeling of an internal conflict. That was the day when he first became aware of the fighting going on in his head between the *Inside Ed* and the *Outside Ed*. It was as if he were two beings rolled into one. His mind was as much a battlefield as Gettysburg. The *Inside Ed* felt stifled, and struggled with the fear of being discovered in his hiding place because if he was recognized he might be required to lead or act in some way - like John Brown. Ed knew the song about John Brown lying in the grave. John Brown was executed, and *Inside Ed* did not want to be placed in the position of opposing the majority; he was not a John Brown. The *Inside Ed* was concerned with what other people saw in him every time he emerged; therefore, he spent most of his time imprisoned deep in the dungeon of denial. Still on occasion, *Inside Ed* found the nerve to escape from his hiding place to do something he felt was right, albeit only covertly, as he did on the day of the accident.

The *Outside Ed* fought for the dominance of Ed O'Reilly's mind; he was the smiling, happy go lucky, carefree personality that enjoyed being accepted by his friends and relatives. *Outside Ed* did not think his own thoughts; he always chose the path of least resistance. As long as he wasn't the instigator, his position regarding racial and social issues was - 'It's not my responsibility.' It was fear that controlled both *Inside Ed* and *Outside Ed* for different reasons; a fear that was hidden under the skin, but a fear nonetheless. Neither of these personalities was free, and their fight for the control of Ed O'Reilly's mind felt like pure pandemonium under his skull.

* * *

Little Jazmine was nearly two years old when her father, J.K. had to come home to bury her mother. After the funeral, J.K. went back to base. When his enlistment time was up, J.K. re-enlisted in the army for an additional two years; however, when he finished his second stint in the service he still didn't come home. He wrote his sister...

> Dearest Illanna,   *January 1945*
> *I thank you for everything you have done for me. Taking care of Jazmine and all. I am finished with the army now. Please excuse me for not coming home right now. I love you, and I love Jazmine, but I can't bear to be so close to where the accident that took my love was. I know I have to be strong for my daughter, but I'm not strong yet, please forgive me. I will keep in touch.*
>
>   *Love, J.K*

When J.K.'s daughter, Jazmine, was about thirteen years old she went to Oliver Shaw's farm to deliver some string beans. Big Mom always shared the bounty from her garden with her neighbors. Jazmine ran those errands often; she always took a short cut through the corn

71

field. On her way back home, Jazmine went the same path. Suddenly, someone grabbed Jazmine from behind, threw her down, and brutally attacked the beautiful child.

Illanna heard a loud piercing scream, but she couldn't discern its source; still Illanna identified the pure horror of the sound. The buckets of string beans Illanna had been snapping flew in the air and exploded like an array of pellets onto the ground... Illanna ran. Her short stubby legs were hardly able to keep up with her body as she darted through the vegetable garden... Illanna ran toward the horror. Oliver Shaw ran toward the corn field when he too heard the scream. Oliver and Illanna reached Jazmine almost simultaneously. They found Jazmine sprawled on the ground, among broken corn stalks; her clothes were torn and bloody, her body was curled up in the fetal position... Her screams were intermittently punctuated by feeble gasps for air... Jazmine kept her eyes squeezed shut; she kicked and struck out as Illanna and Oliver attempted to touch her.

"Child, it's me, it's Big Mom... Let me hold you..." Illanna said softly as she tried to comfort her young niece through her own tears.

"Oh Lord, who did dis ta you!" said Oliver. His entire body shook with the toxin of the suppressed anger he always managed to keep stored just under his skin... Oliver's body shook uncontrollably.

Ed, who was unaware of the flanking wicked event, was driving down Price Road on that same day when he observed a sight that defeated analysis. Ed saw Leaksville's bank president, Mr. Richard McDonald, on horseback as he entered onto the highway from one of the dirt paths not far from Oliver Shaw's farm.

It was not unusual to see a horse on the roadway. Ed's mail car always shared the roadway with horses, horse drawn wagons, school buses, Leaksville public transportation buses, cars, tractors, and people walking on hot summer days with big straw hats and umbrellas. Price Road was busy all day, every day. Ed noticed Mr. McDonald because he never saw the bank president ride a horse before that day.

Initially, Ed didn't think much about seeing Dick McDonald on horseback; however, after reflection, Ed realized something was strange. He wondered... What was that piercing sound he heard shortly before he saw the uncommon horseback rider? Was it a scream? Who? Why?

Ed stored that tid-bit of awareness in his memory, along with the time. Ed was aware of the time that day because he was always aware of time whenever he was working.

Soon Ed noticed little Jazmine constantly sitting on the porch; she didn't seem to play with her cousins any longer. Jazmine sat motionless on the porch, day after day, with her hands limp in her lap; her head bowed low - almost at rest on her chest. She didn't even wave or look up when Ed drove the mail car by. Months passed, and Ed became aware that the dear child was pregnant. Jazmine looked terribly dejected and delicate as her little body expanded.

The church ladies also noticed the child's pregnancy; they called Jazmine and Illanna to an inquisition type meeting. It was the church ladies' intention to make Jazmine apologize publicly to the entire congregation of the church for her sinful ways - which evidentially lead to her pregnancy. Jazmine, Illanna, and Iris (who insisted on going to the meeting too) sat and listened silently to the church ladies' admonitions. Then, without saying a word, Illanna took Jazmine's hand and led the child out of the church. When Illanna stormed out of the church, Iris was right beside her. Iris heard her mother mumble out of her clinched teeth,

"Got some **snake-ey** people round here, hiding in de wood so az you don't know dey there... Yes sir - just a little snake-ey!" Illanna inhaled and then let out one loud, deep breath; her full chest looked as if it might burst.

"Sometimes de church people makes a lot of unchristian rules... Same az a pile of wood, de church is sometimes a safe haven fo' snakes ta hide!" she said.

The day Jazmine's baby boy was born Ed noticed someone, who was a stranger to him, riding on a horse with its tail in intricate knots. Ed was curious about the unconventional horseback rider when he saw her ride down Price Road toward Black Bottom.

"I saw a woman, who was dressed sort of odd; she was riding a horse with its tail knotted. She came this way. Is she someone who lives down in Black Bottom?" Ed asked Nardu the next time he saw him.

"Oh, you must have seen Miss Hag." Nardu said with a strange smile.

"Who is that? I don't have no mailbox up here for a 'Miss Hag'." said Ed.

"She live down in back of Black Bottom. She been there long az I can r'member. Ain't in nobody's family… She stay by herself… She don't use no mailbox, don't write nobody 'n don't nobody write her… But, she always know everything she need ta know. They say she'a decendent of Lilith." Nardu said.

Ed was extremely curious; he never heard of nobody named Lilith, and he thought he knew everybody around here.

"Lilith? Who is Lilith?" Ed asked.

"The story is that Lilith waz the first wife of Adam 'fore da Lord gave 'm Eve." Nardu replied. "Adam didn't like Lilth because: she walked around the garden without him, she did whatever she wanted ta do without asking him, and she wanted ta be on top. Eve's disposition was more ta Adam's liking… Story might be true 'cause Miss Hag sho nuff have her own ways. " Nardu continued.

"Well, I guess I don't know her; that was way before I waz delivering the mail." Ed interrupted and laughed at what he thought was a good joke.

"I don't know how old she is, but she can read people's future." A very serious Nardu replied. "She can even put hexes on somebody if ya need it… I just know one thing; I don't get in Miss Hag's way, 'n I sleep on ma stomach!" Nardu said.

"Why?" asked curious Ed - his levity gone.

"Cause, I heard if a spirit come ta get you in the night, while you sleep, it'll sit on yo'r chest; it'll stop ya from breathing… Spirits attack when yo're on your back." Nardu said.

"What has that got ta do with Miss Hag? She ain't no spirit is she?" Ed asked.

"Can't say she is… Can't say she ain't… But, I ain't taking no chances." Nardu answered with as much honesty as he knew.

Jazmine's baby looked almost White; Ed put two and two together. He remembered the day he saw Mr. McDonald horseback riding, and Ed realized who Jazmine's baby's father was.

"Am I the only one who knows what Mr. McDonald did?" Ed asked his wife.

"No! Of course not!" Ed answered his own question. "Big Mom, Perry, Iris, Oliver Shaw, and Jazmine all know, but they haven't said anything..."

"Ed, you know why." his wife, Suellen, said.

It did not take much deep thinking for Ed to figure out why... It was obvious. The baby grew, and the entire Colored community surmised that the esteemed Mr. McDonald was Jasmine's child's father. Even the church ladies made a special visit to see Illanna and Jazmine; they wanted to express their sorrow because they jumped to conclusions too soon.

"Honey we so sorry, we just didn't know... We thought..." one fair complexioned church lady said as her entire body countenance tried to repeat what her words uttered... "Believe me, I understand..." the light skinned church lady repeated over and over.

"I know what ya'll thought!" Illanna said, with her head held high and both hands on her full hips. "But ya'll were wrong weren't ya? Ma Jazmine is a good girl, 'n God knew that all along - even if ya'll didn't."

Illanna forgave the church ladies; she didn't even resist their gentle and compassionate hugs, but she found no reason to return to church. Illanna decided she would spend her time talking directly to the Lord.

"Such judgmental people might cause interference in ma own direct line of communication with God." Illanna said to her family. She smiled to herself as she thought of God as electricity...

"After all," Illanna said to Perry, "isn't God da great unseen power dat's all 'round us. He's de power dat provides de light of life - once we learn how ta make de connection with'im - without int'rference." Illanna knew Jazmine and her baby boy needed her undivided attention and prayers; the beautiful girl was not the same since she was attacked. The church ladies' visit did not help.

There was talk around town about the baby, but not too loud; however, if Mrs. McDonald ever saw the child there would be no doubt in her mind that Jazmine's baby was the spitting image of Mr. McDonald. Dick McDonald heard of the birth, but he avoided contact and never actually set eyes on little Jarrah Sage. There was one time that he did see Illanna and a young child walking down Washington Street; they went into Belks store. Dick was caught completely off guard as he was coming out of the bank; his heart felt as if it was going to pound out of his body. He realized that Illanna didn't see him, so he turned around and went back into the bank as fast as he could. But, try as he might Dick McDonald could not control his physical reaction. His wiped his palm across his sweaty forehead; then he saw that darn scar on his hand, and the floor seemed to convulse under him. A customer who was leaving the bank asked Mr. McDonald, "Are you okay?" Dick somehow managed a weak "Yes" reply.

J.K. Sage did not come home when his grandchild was born, no one knew where he was; therefore, he didn't know Jarrah existed for an entire year. It was probably best that J.K. didn't know what had happened - somebody would have gotten killed. But, the sad part was that J.K. never got to see Jazmine as a beautiful, healthy daughter because she was more like a walking ghost since she was raped.

Ed remembered how cute baby Jarrah was when he started to walk, and how Jarrah tried to help Illanna take care of his traumatized mother. When J.K. first returned home, he was oblivious to both his daughter and grandson. However, gradually, Ed noticed a subtle change in J.K; he started to show signs of life whenever little Jarrah was around. There were even some days when J.K. came out of his stupor to help Perry work the crops. Maybe Illanna was right about the direct-to-God approach. Illanna and Perry were both dead and gone, but it seemed as if her prayers were actually being answered – slowly but surely.

The childless Elizabeth McDonald's attitude appeared to be - "What I don't know won't hurt me." Besides, Mrs. McDonald never found any joy in her husband's lovemaking; it seemed to be just another way he displayed his selfishness. It was Dick McDonald's style about everything, including sex.

"God gave us de urge fo' sex so we could 'go forth and multiply,' and since I'm past de child bearing age, sex don't matter ta me." Elizabeth told her sister-in-law, Sally, who never said a mumbling word.

Sally was a virgin when she married Allen, and she had so many questions about sex that she dared not ask anyone. What was *it* suppose to feel like? How often did couples do *it?* How did she get pregnant when all she remembered was waking up because Allen was fumbling at the back of her body while she slept on their wedding night? Why did Allen tell her that he loved her too much to ask her to do such nasty things like other men expected from their wives? Was that a sensuous movement she observed when Allen put his hand on his best friend Gregory's knee, or was it her imagination? If sex was so nasty, why did God make the world go 'round on a sexual wheel (birds and bees, pollen and seeds, the reproduction of every species)? All of those questions were never spoken out loud by Sally; most times they stayed in her head, but some times they trickled down into her heart. Every week the doctor reassured Sally that her heart palpitations were anxiety related, not heart trouble.

*   *   *

Freesia Holly went to work, at the McDonald home, early every Monday morning to do the week's wash. The laundry room was next to the kitchen where Lora Berry did the cooking, so the two ladies shared current community information through an ongoing conversation as they worked and observed Elizabeth and Sally in their frustration.

The McDonalds had the latest model Kenmore washing machine, and most times Freesia sneaked some of her own family's laundry in with the Monday wash; otherwise Freesia had to hand wash the laundry for her family on a washboard in a tin tub.

"De old elbow grease is de closest thing ta a modern washing machine dat I own." Freesia said to Lora as she put her own wash load into the machine. Mrs. McDonald knew what Freesia was doing, but she never mentioned it; however, Mr. McDonald would have put a stop to it if he even suspected.

"If ya give a Nigger 'n inch he'll take a mile. Ya can't do him no favors!" was the typical statement Mrs. McDonald could rely on her husband to make as his reaction to any suggestion of kindness toward Colored people. Whereas, Mrs. McDonald was so benevolent that she allowed Freesia to work from home every Tuesday - ironing day. And, every Wednesday Freesia delivered all the ironed laundry by the time the Morning Glories bloomed. The arrangement allowed Freesia a little extra time at home to be a good mother for her own two mischievous children, who were very close in age to Ed's children.

Freesia Holly's husband, Bob, left her for another woman while their children were very young. Although they were still legally married, Bob lived near Greensboro, on Route 29, with his new woman and her children. His visits were spasmodic and did not concur with any child's birthday, special event, or Christmas; actually, Bob only came to visit his children about twice a year. The total responsibility for the children was left on Freesia because her husband contributed very little toward their support – financially or otherwise. Freesia and the children lived their lives as if their husband / father didn't exist. "His not being 'ere would be easier ta 'ccept if'n he had actually died." Freesia said to Lora.

Ed learned all about Freesia's marital conditions and hardships through their long conversations as she stood by her mailbox every Tuesday. Freesia Holly lived at the end of Price Road, near Stoneville; her mailbox was Ed's last stop on his route. Ed looked forward to talking with Freesia before he started his return trip back into town. They talked easily about everything - like old friends.

Freesia once mentioned to Ed that the McDonalds had separate bedrooms.

"Mrs. McDonald said de two bedroom arrangement was best because of her illness… Personally, I think she has a' illness because of de Mr." laughed Freesia.

Yet when their friendship began, both Ed and Freesia were self conscious of the traffic flow on Price Road. They kept their conversations to a respectable time, without really knowing what that time limit was. Those were the days when there was a conflict in Ed's soul… The *Inner Ed* always showed his presence when Ed's brain got a reoccurring question… Why do you care about what other people think? And the

Outer Ed answered the brain question. You don't want to be called a 'N----- lover do you? You know what THEY will say.

The *Inner Ed* kept interjecting thoughts into his brain about a lot of things Ed did not want to think about. For example, the *Inner Ed* actually felt a judgmental anger about the actions of Dick McDonald, who was a representative of Leakesville's high society – such as it was in such a small town. Meanwhile, the *Outer Ed* argued in Ed's head that such feelings were wasted emotions. Nothing Ed felt about Dick McDonald made a ham-fat of difference about the horrible thing that happened to little Jazmine. Still, it was hard for Ed to contain the anger that swelled inside him – to ignore the *Inner Ed* that pounded to be noticed.

Ed continued to drive down the road, pass J.K.'s trailer, with a deep feeling of remorse. He wondered… Was *Outer Ed* ever right? Why were we always so accepting, without thought, when THEY said, "*Things are like they are…*"

The church ladies said… "*In order to make a change one must come face to face with that which needs to be changed.*"

The old folks said, "*Life must be understood backward before we can understand how to live forward.*"

Delphine Greene

Ed drove pass the Spring Baptist Church at the intersection of Price Road and Shady Grove Road; he saw old Deacon Riley as he swept inside the empty church. As a Deacon of the church, he continually looked for ways to serve God's people, so Deacon Riley volunteered to clean the church ten years ago. Every week when he cleaned the church, Deacon Riley felt he was performing a good service; he was confident that God would bless him because of his unselfish work.

Deacon Riley lived nearby with his daughter Delphine, the church organist, and her children. Delphine's husband, Haywood, had been away from Leaksville for so long that Delphine couldn't remember precisely when he left; she only remembered how and why. Her children were only two and three years old when Haywood ran out of town; they don't really remember their father…

Delphine and the children were asleep one summer night when Haywood ran into the house as if he was running from the Devil; he was acting in such fervor that she thought all Hell had broke loose. Haywood hurriedly kissed Delphine and the children telling them,

"I gotta get outta here; I be in touch… I gotta go 'fore anyone get here… dey'll kill me!"

"If anybody ax 'bout me, tell dem you don't know… I lov ya… But, I gotta go!" Haywood groaned into Delphine's ear as he hugged her extra tight. His muscular arms squeezed her so hard that he almost took her breath away… Delphine couldn't say anything; she just stood by, shaking like a leaf on a tree in autumn. She watched her husband scurry about the house - shoving a few articles of clothing into a small hard suitcase as he prepared to run out of her life.

Haywood Greene was never a church-going man; he liked to hang with the party people, and he liked to drink a little bit. Delphine never could get Haywood to give up the moonshine, or the beer.

"A little liquor is good fo' ya," Haywood told his wife. "It's a protection... keeps you from catching a cold. Liquor is a' antib'otic, it keep you from gett'ng sick." he said as he opened another bottle of beer.

Delphine didn't know what to say to Haywood to contradict his statement; she had to admit that Haywood had never been sick as long as she had known him. His physical fortitude could not be disputed; Haywood never caught a cold, even when everybody around him was sick. He worked hard all week, and he drank hard every weekend.

Haywood got into a little trouble before that night, but it was nothing compared to what he was running from then. That Friday night, Haywood and his best friend, Florian Ross, a cousin of Natan Ross, were drinking beer under the stars. It was a warm night, and the two were just hanging out; they were sitting outside of Florian Ross' barn when they heard a noise in the bushes. Florian and Haywood turned around at the same instant - just in time to see two White men walking, out of the woods, toward them.

Florian stood up slowly; he said, "Hello, c'n I help ya Sirs?" as polite as he could; just like he was supposed to - as a non-threatening Negro.

"What ya'll Niggers doing out here 'n de dark?" a voice said.

"Just trying ta gett'a little cool air Sirs." Florian answered while he and Haywood passed apprehensive glances between each other.

As the White men came closer, out from the shadows, Haywood and Florian noticed simultaneously that the men were holding long 2"x 4" boards behind their backs. Neither Haywood nor Florian was inclined to allow themselves to be beaten; then, the men came closer. And, without provocation, they began to swing the boards at Haywood and Florian. As one entity, Haywood and Florian leaped out of the way of the directed hit; then, it was as if the constraint of living under Jim Crow Laws all their lives suddenly burst out of their drunken souls... They confiscated the 2" x 4" boards, and whipped those two White men to a pulp... Haywood and Florian didn't start the fight, but they finished it. When all their energy and frustration was spent, the two friends stood – stunned - in amazement at what they had done. All was quite... Somewhere in the trees an owl, on a solitary vigil, made a long-winded "Who-o-o-o-o." Then, real fear set in!

"Oh Lawd... What we gonna do?" Suddenly, they were no longer drunk...

"We in trouble now!"

In complete silence, yet in a coordinated effort, Haywood and Florian pulled the two limp bodies deep down into the woods, and covered them as best they could with bushes and branches. Then, Haywood and Florian ran faster than their feet could carry them. They ran as if they were no longer contained by human capabilities; they were the Cheetahs ahead of the hunt. They ran to Florian's house first, put some clothes into his old Ford pick up; then, determined to escape the natural confinement of minutes, they drove to Haywood's home - stopping only for a moment to be sick on the side of the road.

Florian waited impatiently in the truck while Haywood ran into his house to get some clothes. Haywood was sweating, water dripped from his body as if he was coming from a swim; his eyes bulged akin to Mantan Molin's display of fear. He looked as if he was going to shake out of his own skin as he said a fretful goodbye to Delphine and his children. The two drinking buddies drove off, rambling at first without direction, through the dark back country roads. They frantically made plans while they were on the move; therefore, Haywood and Florian did not develop escape plans due to any real focus - just real fear...

It was nearly a month before Delphine figured out what may have scared Haywood so much that he abruptly self banished himself from his family and the land of his birth. Delphine heard, through the grapevine, that two decomposed bodies were found in the woods by a farmer on a rabbit hunt. The hunter stepped onto what he thought was splintered wood. When he realized he had stepped on a dead body instead, the scream he emitted was heard throughout Rockingham County. Soon the woods were inundated by the Leaksville Sheriff's department.

Delphine listened to the radio and read the newspapers; she absorbed all the news she could about the case. Delphine felt the split ends of every nerve in her body... The word around town was that the dead men were from Stoneville; Leaksville residents didn't know them. The lackadaisical Leaksville Sheriff didn't have a clue as to what may have happened. The waiting, the not knowing, was hard for Delphine to bear; she couldn't discuss her concerns with anyone, not her pastor, not her friends, not even her father. Delphine cried alone…

The murder investigation did not yield any results; therefore, the sheriff concluded that the two men had been murdered elsewhere and dumped in his jurisdiction. A few years later, after a nonchalant investigation, the sheriff closed the case without arresting or charging anyone.

Delphine explained to her neighbors that her husband and Florian had gone up North get jobs; no-one knew exactly when they left, so they were never suspects in the murders. Nevertheless, Florian and Haywood were still afraid to come back home… They never did return.

Deacon Riley, a widower, came to live with his daughter. And, Delphine resigned herself to being satisfied with the occasional letters from Haywood as he moved from one place to another before he ended in Philadelphia. He and Florian lost touch with each other shortly after their escape. While they were on the run, it became every man for himself. They went their separate ways… Although Florian's family tried to find him, they never heard from him again.

Haywood had already left home when Ed became the mailman; thus, Ed never met Haywood. Ed only knew about Haywood because of the excitement Delphine Greene could not contain when she realized a letter he delivered was from her husband. Ed began to recognize Haywood's handwriting on the envelope - even if the return address was different. Delphine always had a sad, yet dreamy, look whenever she opened Haywood's letters; sometimes she shared a memory with Ed.

"My Haywood is a smart man; he likes ta read. Dis package I'm mailing ta him is some of his favorite books; I figure he would like ta have dem. You know he graduated at de top of his high school class – had da brains ta go ta college, but he didn't hav' no college money." Delphine told Ed as she handed him the package to be mailed.

There were nights when Delphine couldn't sleep at all, and her pillow offered no comfort. After a few years, Delphine saved up enough money to go to Philadelphia; it was the first time she and Haywood had seen each other since that dreadful night he left. Delphine eagerly planned for the trip, she: made new clothes, bought new lingerie, got her hair done at the beauty shop - instead of doing it herself, bought hat and gloves to match her favorite dress, and purchased a new suitcase.

When Delphine returned from the trip, a week later, all her friends and neighbors were excited for her and extremely inquisitive.

"Girl, are you gonna move up North?"

"You better go stay with Haywood. You know you can't leave a good man too long… Some sweet thang gonna get him!"

"Wish my man had a job up North… I'd sho nuff be with him… Yes mam, wouldn't have to ask me twice!"

Delphine wished her friends would leave her alone, and mind their own business! She knew they meant well, but those friends were getting on her last nerve! Delphine knew, absolutely, that she would never move up North with Haywood; in fact, if he didn't come back to Price Road, they would never be together again. After her experience on her trip to Philly, Delphine knew she was never even going to visit Haywood again.

When Delphine arrived at the Greyhound Bus Station, on Market Street in downtown Philadelphia, she tried not to look disheveled. It had been a long bus ride. Delphine's rump needed to be fluffed, and her legs and arms ached as they were reminded of their natural position. The bus had stopped at all the small towns and storefront stations along Routes 1 and 13. The fried chicken Delphine brought with her, in a shoebox, was finished somewhere around Washington, D.C.. Riding in the back of the bus had made her nauseous from the bouncing rear wheels and excessive exhaust fumes; additionally, there was a man, who sat near the middle of the bus, with a half smoked cigar in his mouth. The smell from the cigar was horrible, even though the man was not actually smoking; consequently, when Delphine arrived in Philadelphia she felt queasy, and her bladder alerted her to the necessity of a visit to the bathroom.

Delphine was overjoyed when her bus reached its destination; it was the awaited moment. Delphine tried to look calm as she slowly stepped off the bus while her innards seemed to galvanize their own opposition forces. Her eyes slowly scanned over the crowd - looking for Haywood. He was nowhere to be seen. Delphine was afraid to leave the waiting area; she didn't want to miss Haywood because she had gone to the bathroom. Although it was difficult to control her body impulses, Delphine adjusted her hat, crossed her legs, and sat on her suitcase for at least an hour before she spotted her husband walking toward her.

Delphine could always spot Haywood; she knew his walk: the little hesitation of his left foot as he stepped forward, the slight bow of his right leg below the knee barely causing a distinguishing limp. Delphine's heart leaped into her throat when she spotted her man walking in her direction.

When Haywood hugged her, he planted a firm kiss on her lips and mumbled an apology for being late. Delphine melted in his arms. Delphine closed her eyes to feel the rippling muscles - the strength and firmness of the arms she missed. Instead she seemed to fold into an unwashed shirt, draped on a wire clothes hanger; the muscles were gone, and there was a musty odor. The combination of excessive cigarette smoke, stale liquor, and a fishy body odor that encircled Haywood made Delphine gag. The unexpected decadence of her senses caused Delphine's heart to throb in a hurtful way. She pinched her lips together and secured them tightly, with her teeth, from the inside. Delphine held her breath… She couldn't speak…

Haywood lived in a large three story brick house, on North Broad Street, with a large front porch and high ceilings; it was originally built for one family. In its day, it was a superb building with a beautiful combination of brick, stone, and delicately crafted woodwork; its fine workmanship was comparable to a mini mansion. Any visions of debutantes and gents in fine dress (standing on the large porch, or leaning on the marble mantel over the carved imported stone fireplace) must have been real at one time. But, years later, the elegance was gone. The house as it stood in a row, alongside similar structures, reminded Delphine of an old man who has lost his youth and teeth. It was one of the many rooming houses within several city blocks of crumbling decay. Haywood rented a furnished room in the house; it was the front room on the second floor.

Haywood held Delphine's' hand as they gingerly stepped over a drunk man on the front steps, another fuzzy looking drunk was laying in the doorway. Delphine's world twirled, it was as if she were trying to cross a swamp without stepping or falling on the sleeping 'gators lying in the water. What was she stepping into? They passed through enormous double doors that could have very well have been the gates of Hell. Delphine followed her husband into a long dark hallway. The rickety staircase creaked as they climbed to the second floor; in the process Delphine had to avoid stepping on two… three 'gators. The walls were layered with faded and torn wallpaper, and patches of paint. A horrible, unbearable smell of urine penetrated every corner of the building. Delphine held her gloved hand over her nose and mouth… Her breath seemed as if it had been snatched away. People in the house were constantly coming and going, in and out of the slamming doors, running, stumbling, falling, yelling, fighting… And, always loud!

Everybody shared the same bathroom and kitchen facilities. An animal, that may have been a German Shepard dog, lay near one of the 'gators. The animal's large eyes looked up as Delphine and Haywood walked by; the creature, which seemed to lick a wounded paw, looked more dead than alive. Rats casually walked around the house night and day, down the halls, in and out of the rooms, on the tables and counters in the kitchen; they crawled over the drunken bodies without fear. Roaches were everywhere, they hung from the once beautiful chandelier, they fell off the walls to dance on the warped, pee stained hardwood floors… Delphine cringed.

A sagging double bed sat between the two long, narrow front windows in Haywood's room. Delphine walked slowly, past the bed, toward the windows; then, she stopped firmly in place. The bare windows stared at her like the cloudy blue, unseeing eyes of someone blind. Delphine was speechless…

There was no-where to sit except on the bed. The stained mattress was so lumpy it appeared to be filled with straw. Visions of her childhood leaped forth; the tender, affectionate, bedtime song her, father sang to her, pounded brutally in Delphine's head.

"Good night, sleep tight,
Don't let the bed bugs bite"

Delphine stood in place and looked around... Somehow she managed to contain the tears.

"So, what chu think?" Haywood asked. "Not bad, huh?"

Delphine tried to manage a smile for Haywood. She noted the fact that his skin had the same fuzzy look as the sleeping drunk 'gator, in the doorway; it was the indescribable look that betrays a system too full of alcohol. Therefore, it didn't matter how much Haywood told her that he had stopped drinking; his skin gave him away.

Delphine was impatient to go back home; to stay the entire week was the hardest thing she ever did. She could not lie down and go to sleep; she sat every night at the head of the bed, arms around her knees, lights on, and her eyes alert for every movement.

"Delphine honey, why don't you lie down and go ta sleep? Are ya so excited to be in de city dat you'r scared ta sleep? Scared ya gonna miss something?" Haywood asked.

"Yes, guess ya right, ain't never seen nothing like dis here city." she replied.

Actually, the minute Delphine saw where she had to stay, she felt like turning around and taking the next bus back to North Carolina. Delphine had not considered bringing the children with her because she was looking forward to spending time alone with her husband; indeed, as she considered the circumstances, Delphine realized how right the decision had been.

"I wish ya could hav' brought da children. I'm disappointed 'bout not seeing dem." Haywood told her.

An uncontrollable loneliness and depression germinated in the empty space in Haywood's soul. He remembered the good times he had with his children. He always read them bedtime stories, brushed their hair, and showed his boys how to go to the toilet – just like dad... He remembered the days Delphine sat on the porch and watched him play ball, in the backyard, with their boys. Haywood could still almost feel the children's body weight as they jumped on him when he returned home from a hard day's work in the fields; it was as if the cells in his body refused to forget. In his depression, Haywood thought - maybe more drinks would help...The alcohol initially worked as a camouflage - a shield against feelings, against thoughts... Haywood became an analytical person; sometimes, in his drunken stupor Haywood tried to understand '*Life*.' In a conversation, with a group of drinking buddies, Haywood once remarked,

"You know what life is? I'll tell you what life is," Haywood said. He pronounced every syllable in every word. Haywood tried to speak in the vernacular of a professor - even though he had difficulty holding his head up.

"Life is like a progression, like a journey, like you traveling on a road – trying to get somewhere without a map… Every decision a person makes can reset the course. You know - alter the direction. Just a little bit in the beginning. It's like the road of life is full of forks…Yep, the old fork in the road… All your life you always deciding which fork to take… You never sure which is the right fork… When you decide to take a fork that leads you away, it's hard to go back... You know – Like it's hard to change a bad decision in life. It's impossible to unscramble scrambled eggs!" The intoxicated pseudo professor Haywood said to his buddies as his unsteady hands became additional parts of speech. Haywood spent a lot of time in solitude; during those times he wondered when, where, and what was the decision in his life that resulted in the lost of his family - that sent him out to sea alone - without a paddle.

Delphine was so glad that she hadn't brought the children with her, children should never be exposed to this type of life style; although, she was aware that there were children who lived in this rooming house, she was so happy they were not hers. Haywood tried his best to make sure Delphine was comfortable during her visit; he tried not to drink, and he almost succeeded. He only got drunk one night during Delphine's stay.

"I'll be right back." Haywood said as he left Delphine that last night. She sat cringing on middle of the bed all night. Haywood didn't return until the next morning; he tried to apologize with a hug and kiss. Delphine silently pushed him away - disgusted. The pronounced smell of stale wine was more than she could take. Haywood fell, in a stupor, across the lumpy bed. Delphine made an effort to keep him awake; she could not. Haywood began to snore – a deep gurgling noise with intermittent pauses. Delphine gave up - she took her suitcase and tiptoed out of the room. She found her way to the Broad Street Subway, and asked the ticket collector for directions to the Greyhound bus station. While Delphine waited for the bus bound for North Carolina, she bought some bug spray; her skin still felt as if things were crawling on her.

Delphine thought about a joke her father loved to tell about two men driving down the road. The driver asked his passenger to check the traffic on his right so that he could drive across an intersection.

"Is there anything coming?" the driver asked.

"Nothing but a dog…" The passenger answered calmly. Then, suddenly their car was hit by a large bus, and crushed with a horrible force.

"I thought you said nothing was coming but a dog!" The angry driver screamed at his passenger.

"Oh, did I forget to say it was a **Greyhound**?" The slow talking passenger said.

Delphine felt as if she had collided with a Greyhound bus; she was emotionally bruised, crushed, and trodden. Delphine looked out of the window of the big Greyhound bus; finally, fatigue overcame her resistance, and she fell asleep. Delphine's mind was already firmly made up… *That was her last trip to Philadelphia!*

Whenever anybody back home asked Delphine about her trip to Philly, or her husband, Delphine just smiled. When necessary, she replied with her preplanned statement,

"Haywood's doing fine… He gotta job, just don't pay enough for me 'n da kids ta join'm yet, won't be long… He working real hard… Doing good… Sho nuf… Doing good…"

Delphine told Ed the same story; however, Ed noticed that the return address on the letters, from Haywood, kept changing as regularly as the seasons for planting and harvesting tobacco. Meanwhile, Delphine planted a flower garden of pink and red carnations, and forget-me-not's. Delphine viewed the flower garden in a symbolic way. On Mother's Day people wore pink and red carnations to acknowledge love for a mother who was still alive; white carnations honored a mother who was deceased. The colors in Delphine's garden reflected her feelings, she was caught somewhere between life and death. She vowed that she would think of Haywood whenever she looked at her flowers; she tried to think positively, to put something beautiful into an ugly situation. Delphine never forgave Haywood for putting her life in such a state of affairs, yet she never forgot him. Sometimes, when she looked at the flowers, Delphine actually doubled over with an agonizing pain; in addition, sometimes night terrors interrupted her sleep. The separation was hard for her, and she felt angry that Haywood allowed himself to slide down the slippery slope. She prayed…

"Don't Haywood love us 'nough to get himself t'gether? Please help him." Delphine asked of God. She tried not to make her request in the form of a demand.

The year after her Philadelphia visit, Delphine redecorated her house. She wrapped Haywood's pictures carefully in newspaper, and cautiously placed all of them together out of harm's way into a small trunk; then, she cried after she increased the Metropolitan life insurance policy she and Haywood had gotten shortly after they got married.

Delphine did not let the children forget that they had a father although as time passed it was easier not to speak of him as often. After awhile Haywood's letters stopped coming as frequently; then, the letters stopped altogether. Delphine never stopped writing to Haywood; eventually her letters were returned with no forwarding address. Delphine never spoke to anyone about the returned letters; nevertheless, she thought about what might happen to the bodies of the unknown, the unclaimed, or the lost and missing dead in Philadelphia. Delphine wondered… How would she know?

The old folks said… *It's a sad soul that don't have a pot to piss in, or a window to throw it out of.*

Delphine understood…

The church ladies said… *It wasn't raining when Noah built the ark.*

ZARA'S ZESTY TREATS

Ed passed a farmer, with a horse drawn wagon full of corn, on his way to the mill near the Hilltop Club where the ears of corn would be ground into cornmeal. It was a common sight for Ed to see the farmers carrying their produce down Price Road, on trucks or wagons, for various reasons: corn or wheat to the mill, pigs to the slaughter house, fruits or vegetables to sell in town, eggs and milk to deliver to regular customers.

Most of the farmers raised one or two pigs yearly, and owned at least one cow. The cow supplied the milk, which could be churned to make butter and buttermilk. The butter was developed into beautiful molds and sold to the townspeople who did not own a cow. Farm families never had any garbage to throw away; they slopped the pigs with a watered mixture of their food residue – nothing went to waste.

The pigs were fattened all summer and taken to the slaughter house in the fall. At the slaughter house the pig was hung on a rack in a cold meat storage locker until it was smoked and cut into hams and shoulders. Each pig was tagged and numbered to insure that it is returned to the right family. It was packaged in thick, individual, loosely woven sacks which were then hung in the family's storehouse (a large wooden building usually located behind the main house). The smoked hams had to be hung - suspended from the rafters, high above everything in the storehouse - an effort to prevent the rats from getting into the meat.

Sometimes Ed bought bushels of apples, peaches, snap beans, or chic peas from the farmers. He took the food home to Suellen; she made preserves, jelly, and pickles. By the time winter took its mighty stand, Suellen always had a storage cupboard full of canned goods, and more in the crawl space under the house. Every winter, especially near Christmas, Ed bought black walnuts and pecans from Iris and Natan Ross, who were the only family on Price Road who had nut trees in their back yard. The Berry family had a lemon and a lime tree on their property, and Freesia Holly and her children sold blueberries from the vines in their backyard. Ed could go home every day with groceries without ever having to go into a grocery store.

Ed felt lucky to have a wife, like Suellen, who did not complain or nag him about all sorts of nonsense; he was not a perfect husband, but she was as close to a perfect wife as one could get. Once Ed said to Fressia, "I don't say she's a smart woman 'cause she chose me fo' her husband, but 'cause she really is; I'm a lucky man." Whenever Ed wanted to give Suellen a special treat, he purchased something from Zara Frasier - who made the best cakes and pies in Rockingham County.

Mrs. Zara was known for her spectacular baking; she lived down the road from the Spring Church, and always donated cakes, pies or tarts to the pot luck dinners. The other women didn't try to compete with her; they stuck to the main course of the meal and left the desserts to Mrs. Zara, with the exception of the homemade ice cream, which became a project for everyone – young and old alike. The entire congregation took turns, as necessary, to rotate the handle on the salt and ice filled, wooden framed, ice cream maker. There was pure excitement and anticipation as the silver inner container, packed with a fresh fruit filled cream mixture, became harder and harder to turn.

The ice cream was ready to eat when the strongest helper couldn't turn the handle on the mixer any more. In the winter, after a good snowfall, the ice cream could be made out of fresh fallen snow. The mothers gathered the fresh snow from roof tops or window sills immediately after the snowfall to avoid the accidental collection of impure snow; in fact, it was not a joke when they warned their children, "Don't eat yellow snow!" Regardless of the flavor source, home made ice cream was everybody's desire; a perfect compliment to Mrs. Zara's baked goods. *Oh goodness!* What a mouth watering time! Everybody stood around, waiting in anticipation, with their bowls and spoons in hand. Children were given the coveted ice cream covered ladle, from the middle of the ice cream maker, as an extra serving reward whenever they helped to turn the handle.

Mrs. Zara learned to cook at her grandmother's elbow. Her grandma cooked without a recipe; she simply measured a pinch of something here, a sprinkle of something there. Zara adapted the same style, and learned to create her own recipes so no-one was able to duplicate anything she made exactly the same way. Many of Zara's special pastry orders came from the well-to-do white women in town... They loved her cooking.

Often Zara was hired to oversee a large dinner or a special social event. Even when there was a cook-of-the-house already employed by the host, Zara unquestionably became the one in charge on those occasions; such was the case in the Ryan household. Sally Ryan was often asked to host large dinner meetings for Allen's associates in his real estate development business, and Zara was always hired to cater the affair. Although Sally was the lady of the house, it was Allen who confirmed Zara's menus and decorating theme choices for such important events.

When they complimented the cook at one of his dinners, Allen Ryan suggested to the owners of the Leaksville's largest general store/ lunch counter that it would be a good business move to carry Zara's homemade cookies and brownies in their store. Zara's reputation for catering and baked goods spread... Other stores, including the Mc-Neil General Store on Price Road, began to retail Zara's baked treats. She placed her baked goods in small plain brown paper bags, with an identifiable label, and the orders started coming faster than Zara could believe. She felt overwhelmed as if she had been caught in a pounding rain from a sudden cloudburst... She needed help.

Zara Frasier's children, Bruce and Buttercup, and her husband Lyndell became her assistants. They helped in the kitchen and made deliveries. Lyndell was a farmer when he married Zara, but when she needed his help with her thriving business he rented his farmland to Mr. Udell's son-in-law and daughter. Ed usually saw Lyndell Frasier, with one of the children, driving their Ford station wagon (with the wooden side panels), up and down Price Road... loaded with baked goods as they made deliveries all during the day. Within a ten year period, Zara and her family developed a financially rewarding baking business.

Zara did not grow up on Price road, Lyndell did. He met her during a dance at the Colored Community Center (CCC), in Reidsville, several years before they married.

The neighbors on Price Road didn't know the stranger that Lyndell showed up with one day. There were a few surprised young ladies and disappointed mothers when Lyndell introduced this fluttering woman from Reidsville, the home of the large Lucky Strike tobacco factory and uppity city sophistication, as his wife. Some of the church ladies had always held marriage hopes for their daughters since Lyndell was the little groom in the Tom Thumb Wedding, years ago.

The church ladies didn't want to like Lyndell's wife; '*they*' found fault with everything she did. '*They*' thought Zara wore too much makeup, laughed too loud, and waved her hands too much when she talked. *They* had known Lyndell from his birth; *they* expected him to do better in selecting a mate, and *they* didn't mind letting that fact be known. Lyndell ignored the old church ladies' subversive comments and showed them that he loved his wife; there was nothing *they* could say to change that fact.

Zara never changed her flamboyant ways, but over the years everyone grew to love her anyway. She was a good wife and mother, and even though she worked from dawn 'til deep into the night she always managed to look like a model. It was her hard work that provided the money for her family to be the first on Price Road to have inside plumbing. After Zara's new bathroom and remodeled kitchen became the talk of Price Road, the church ladies testified to Lyndell about his choice of a 'Godly' wife. He heard their put-on compliments every time they stopped by his house for one of their regular impromptu visits.

"Zara, do you mind if I use your bathroom? Sho' is a nice bathroom!"

"You sho' got yourself a good wife Lyndell"

"Yes s'r God so'nuff done blessed you!"

Zara and Lyndell were always gracious, and demonstrated to their guest how every feature of the new bathroom worked. Inside plumbing was the first step toward an inside toilet - which was everybody's dream. So, the visits to the Frasier household really served as reaffirmation of everybody's dream; it was proof that the dream was within reach, that it was just a matter of time before everybody on Price road could have the same luxury.

The old folks said... *"What ever you can believe you can achieve!"*

The Frasiers didn't need to use the outhouse; yet, they never tore it down. "It's best ta have it 'vailable 'n case something ever goes wrong wid da indoor plumbing... Best ta be safe - not sorry." Zara said to her husband. Therefore, the double seated outhouse continued to stand in the backyard as an insurance statement with an old Sears and Roebuck catalog inside. Ed could see the tin roof of the outhouse from his car; the structure had become a symbol for the merging of past and present on this land.

Ed remembered Lyndell's nephew, Buddy; there was no-one on earth that appreciated the toilet inside the house as much as Buddy. He was about seven years old when he first came from New York to spend the summer with his Uncle Lyndell and his cousins. After a month in the country, Buddy - the city cousin, became very sick with a dangerously high fever. The doctor discovered, through interrogation, that the sick little boy had not been to the toilet to have a bowel movement since he had been in North Carolina - the entire month of July!

"I'm scared to go to the toilet in that outhouse." Buddy cried. "There might be a snake or rat down in that hole! There are spiders in there too! I'm scared to be in there by myself... I just can't go! And, I can't wipe myself with that stiff paper from that Sears catalog!" he whimpered.

The doctor sympathized with the almost hysterical child, and gently explained, "This enema I'm going to give you is going to make you feel better." The doctor assured Buddy that he could use the slop jar without leaving the bedroom.

Little Buddy exploded into the white porcelain slop jar more than once, and he apologized each time to his concerned Uncle Lyndell - who had the repulsive job of disposing of the stinking output. Buddy's parents hurried from New York to get their son; in fact, Buddy did not visit his Uncle Lyndell again until his uncle installed the inside toilet. Buddy's relatives never let him forget the 'summer of the outhouse incident' no matter how old he got to be.

"Boy, remember the year ya almost got locked bowels! Ha- Ha…"

"You scared us to death… Boy, don't no snake want you! See your naked butt 'n a snake'll slither 'way in a hurry!"

None of this was funny to the boy, but he just smiled. Buddy tried to apply the advice he heard from the old men on the porch at the Mc-Neil store. He hoped that if he didn't answer the teasing would stop; usually it did.

The old folks said… *Don't ever let them see you sweat.*

Ed heard about the outhouse incident; it was one of the stories retold at the gathering on the store porch. And, along with everybody else, Ed laughed although he could personally identify with the little boy's trepidation. Ed understood Buddy's fear; he remembered feeling the same way when he was a child although he had to learn to cope with his fears because North Carolina was his home - outhouse and all. There was no-place else to go. Ed thought about his childhood: all the fears he never spoke, the qualms he never expressed, the uncertainties he internalized and carried into adulthood.

"Yes, I know what he went through; I definitely understood Buddy's fear. I guess the more fear you have the more stuff you keep locked up inside of you… Locked-minds can be just as dangerous as locked-bowels. " Ed muttered so softly that the sound of his voice barely reached his own ears, and he decided to stop at Mrs. Zara's to get something sweet… It didn't matter if it was a cake, pie, or cookies; it was going to be a nice treat for his family…

THE KEYS

Ed continued to drive slowly down the road; the next mailbox belonged to Mr. and Mrs. Keys, who were retired educators. Neither of the Keys grew up in Rockingham County. They were both in their twenties, directly out of college, when they started teaching at Leaksville's Douglas High School. Mrs. Keys attended Bennett College for Girls in Greensboro, NC; and Mr. Keys graduated from Hampton Institute - in Hampton, VA. The couple met and fell in love the first year they worked together; they married at Spring Baptist Church in July of their second year of teaching… That was fifty- five years ago.

"You should have seen her. She wore a white silk gown, that she made herself, with a wreath of baby breaths in her hair." Mr. Keys exclaimed. "Yes-sir-ree!" he almost yelped.

"When she seemed to float down the aisle, I said to myself, 'You are one lucky man,' you are marrying an angel!" Mr. Keys stated without reservation.

Mr. Keys talked about the wedding as if it were yesterday; he shook his head in disbelief that this beautiful cinnamon colored woman, with freckles sprinkled across her cheeks, loved and married him. Whenever Mr. Keys told the story, Mrs. Keys smiled while she tilted her head with the poise of a model. Mr. Keys did not consider himself handsome by any standard he knew of; he was always self conscious of that one eye that wouldn't stay in place, no matter how hard he tried. He wore sun glasses most all the time in an effort to camouflage the unusual eye.

Mr. Keys taught Math, and Mrs. Keys taught English. It appeared that the Keys knew something about anything of importance, or they knew how to find the answer to any question; hence, the Price Road neighbors came to this educated couple whenever they needed help that required deeper thinking or understanding.

The Keys did not have children of their own, even though they tried; Mrs. Keys didn't seem to be able to carry a pregnancy to full term. Their home was large and exquisite, with hardwood floors, Oriental rugs, porcelain figurines, highly polished mahogany furniture, and Lenox China. The three bedroom house was purchased because there had once been the unfulfilled hope for children; however, instead of a nursery one entire bedroom, and the area normally used as a dinning room, slowly became additional library space. Books seemed to be everywhere in the Keys' home, from floor to ceiling, and they were organized alphabetically according to the name of the author.

The public library in Leaksville had a small, dim, cubby-hole space in the back, set aside for Colored people to use. Very few of the Negro community used the public library; they felt it was degrading, but it was all that was required under the Jim Crow Laws. Mr. and Mrs. Keys recognized the void and made their personal collection of books available to their neighbors. The mail Ed delivered to the Keys' house always had new books, magazines, maps, or brochures. Mr. Keys invited Ed into their house one day when he delivered a particularly large shipment of World Book Encyclopedias.

"Ed, can you please help me carry this into the house?" Mr. Keys asked.

"Sure Mr. Keys." Ed said.

"The Mrs. and I love good books. You like to read?" Mr. Keys asked while he carried the heavy package toward his house. As Ed followed Mr. Keys through the front door, he shook his head as a positive answer.

When he entered the house, Ed stopped abruptly. He had never seen a home like this before. He found himself standing motionless as his eyes scanned the perimeters. He was in awe of the abundance of books he saw, and the sight captured his voice box… Ed could not make a sound… He could only nod his head, which he did - nonstop.

"Care to look at some?" Mr. Keys gave Ed a welcome-to-look gesture while he enthusiastically tore open the new delivery of books. Ed stood as stationary as a support beam, his eyes roamed from floor to ceiling - over shelves and shelves of books. He saw several sets of encyclopedias on the shelves already. There were rows of: large and small dictionaries, medical, musical, nutritional, scientific, research books, and even an entire wall of children's books.

"Ya'll read all this stuff?" Ed asked in amazement.

"I've got some autographed books that I am very proud of, I keep them over here." Mr. Keys stated as he ushered Ed to the opposite side of the room where he revealed a display of pictures on the ledge over the fireplace. Upon closer inspection, Ed discovered all the pictures were of Mr. or Mrs. Keys, sometimes both, with the author and a copy of a personally signed book.

"That's Zora Neal Hurston; she wrote *Their Eyes Are Watching God*...I think it was her second novel." Mr. Keys informed Ed.

Just then Mrs. Keys came into the room. She was in the kitchen when she overheard the men talking. "Hello Ed." said Mrs. Keys who spoke with a very precise, crisp - yet soft, tone of voice. She articulated each word clearly, every syllable was pronounced to perfection; no-one else along Price Road had a similar speaking style. Even if Ed had not been in her house he would have recognized Mrs. Keyes' voice. He turned toward her and extended his hand.

"Howdy, Mrs. Keys, dis here is some collection ya'll have." Ed said. Mrs. Keys simply gave a proud smile of acknowledged truth.

"You're welcomed to look; in fact, you can borrow one if you would like to read it." Mrs. Keyes offered.

"This is Langston Hughes and his *Montage of a Dream Deferred* that he wrote in 1951. We met him in New York, Harlem, I think in 1952." Mr. Keys said. His body language implied that his vie for attention was good natured.

"This is a picture of James Baldwin with my wife, and the copy of his first novel, *Go Tell It On The Mountain*." Mr. Keys continued. "We went to see his play, *Amen Corner*, when it was performed at Howard University a couple of years ago. Now that we are retired we can travel to enhance and explore the interest that we have in so many things... Right, Mrs. Keys?" Mr. Keys said.

He always called his wife Mrs. Keys; he said it was something he did because he was so happy to have her as his wife. Every time he said, "Mrs. Keys" it reminded him of the reason for his years of happiness. She returned the respect and acknowledged her husband as "Mr. Keys".

"I like baseball, so whenever we can we try to combine our vacation time with a game. You like baseball don't you? Look, here is a picture of me with Jackie Robinson and Roy Campanella!" Mr. Keys held the picture for Ed to get a closer look; then, Ed's eyes connected with other books on a nearby shelf.

"This here's a name I recognize." he said. "Booker T. Washington; he is the only one here that I ever heard of, but I never read anything he wrote." Ed commented as he bent his knees for a new vantage point.

"I'm not surprised, if you don't mind my saying so, he is one Negro that most people have heard of. Would you like to read his autobiography, *Up From Slavery*? Here, I'll let you borrow this one." Mr. Keys said.

"Ok, Yes I'd like to" Ed reached for the book, and flipped through the pages.

"I'll let you sign out for it; that's what I do with everyone who borrows a book from me, and you can keep it for a week."

"You mean you let people borrow your books all the time?" Ed said in astonishment.

"Sure, just keep the book in good condition, and bring it back like we ask; someone else may want to borrow it." Mr. Keys replied.

"Are you saying I can borrow another book when I bring this one back... just like the Leaksville Library does?" Ed asked.

"Mr. Keys you hav' books that I've never seen 'n da Leaksville library. Matter of fact, I don't know of anybody that's got dis many books 'n their home" Ed commented as his eyes continued to scan the shelves around the room.

"Oh absolutely Ed - you are right... That's our intention... Mrs. Keys and I have a great collection of Negro authors and magazines. We also love the classics: Shakespeare, Emerson, Hemmingway, Poe, and lots of others. You will have to come back when you have more time to look." Mr. Keys replied.

Mr. Keyes was always excited whenever someone showed an interest in his books. He was energized as he showed Ed the various books of which he was extremely proud.

"I have Henry Thoreau's *Walden Pond*. Do you know that book is a helpful tool to help teach math? I use the section about *The Bean Field* for that purpose; it helps keep a child interested in the subject when they can see the crossover relationship…You know what I mean?" Mr. Keys said. Just then somebody knocked at the screen door.

"Come in," said Mrs. Keys as she headed toward the door. It was Heather Shaw, Oliver Shaw's teenage daughter.

"Come in honey," said Mrs. Keys. She escorted the child into the room.

"Hi everybody," Heather spoke, acknowledging all present.

"Mrs. Keyes I'm bringing back the copy of *Crisis*, can I get something else?

"Of course you can." Mrs. Keys answered.

"What is that… that *Crisis* she's bringing back?" Ed asked.

"Oh, that's the journal for the N.A.A.C.P. The wife and I are lifetime members. That's just one of the magazines and journals we subscribe to… Want to see it?" Mr. Keys replied. He handed the journal to Ed for him to browse through.

"Come on, let me show you." Mr. Keys proceeded down the hallway. Ed followed into a room full of magazines and newspapers, most of which Ed had never heard of.

Ed discovered that Mr. and Mrs. Keys tutored anybody, adults or children, without charge whenever they were asked; in fact, the Keys house always had a consistent stream of visitors seeking information or confirmation on some subject. The Keyes' excitement about education was contagious. Ed did not register for a class, but he became a student.

The church ladies said… *Wisdom is sweet to your soul if you find it you will have a bright future, and your hope will not be cut short.* Proverbs 24:14

* * *

On his last day as the mailman Ed pulled his mail car into the driveway alongside the Keys' houses. Mrs. Keys, who was looking out her kitchen window, called loudly to her husband.

"Mailman… The mailman is here!"

Elaine T. Jones

They both came to the front door while Ed remained in the car. Mr. Keys came to the driver's side of the car and reached his hand in for a hardy handshake.

"Ed we're sure going to miss you, but you feel free to come on out to see us anytime. You hear?" Mr. Keys said.

"That's right Ed… Anytime…" Mrs. Keys affirmed with a wave from her stance on the front porch. Ed pulled out of the driveway after he handed Mr. Keys the book he most recently borrowed; it was a copy of *David Walker's Appeal.* Ed knew it was one of the Keys most valued possessions; there were very few copies in existence, and he had been extremely careful even when he turned the pages so as to not damage the book in any way.

"Thanks Mr. Keys, I would like to continue to borrow books if you don't mind." Ed said…

Anytime Ed… Anytime." Mr. Keyes replied…

BILL O. WRIGHT

Ed drove on to the next mailbox. The principal of Douglas School, Professor Bill O. Wright and his family, lived in a humble two story home across the road from Mr. and Mrs. Keys. Professor Wright was well known and respected for the work he did at the school. He was very involved with the administrative work, so he seemed to have little time for many one-on-one connections with the people he serviced. Ed found the postmarks on the mail he delivered to Professor Wright's home fascinating because they came from so many places around the world.

The Professor gave the aura of being a critical mind, so well educated and informed about everything, of a keen intelligence; it was a persona that made others, without his educational credentials, tend to feel inferior. Therefore, many of his neighbors were not inclined to go to the Professor for personal help or advice. Nevertheless, all of his neighbors paid tribute to the Professor for the work they knew he did in their behalf.

Ever since Professor Bill O. Wright had been the principal of Douglas School, he did all he could to get the books and supplies for the under-funded school from the Board of Education. Although all the school furnishings and almost all of the books were previously used by the white students, the Professor had to 'shin and grin' and say '*Yessa Mister*'; he held his tongue many more times than his digestive system could take. As a man of culture, Professor Wright controlled his outward expression; that was the easy part. It was hard to control the damaging effects that the deep, unexpressed, utterly consuming emotions had on his nucleus; consequently, the Professor suffered from high blood pressure, diabetes, and celiac disease.

"Professor, you got to watch what you eat… Stay away from sugar. You can eat rice and corn, but don't eat anything made with oats, or wheat." Mr. Vera advised after a sick spell kept the Professor home-bound for a week.

"You know what I think?" Mr. Vera continued as he wagged his finger toward the ailing Professor. "I think you like a pressure cooker that's about to blow it's top; you got to stop holding all that stuff inside. Maybe you could just go out in the woods by yourself and scream sometimes if you 'fraid of somebody knowing you have feelings." Mr. Vera boldly suggested - knowing that his seniority in age gave him certain liberties with the Professor that others would never have taken.

"I'm going to give you some homework," Mr. Vera said with a broad grin. "Here... I want you to read this book" he said as he handed the Professor a copy of *East of Eden.* "This is possibly the most important thousand pages you could ever read in your life."

The Professor accepted the book; he appreciated the thought, and he tried to follow Mr. Vera's advice amidst his strenuous schedule. Professor Bill O. Wright did not like feeling so unhealthy, so out of shape, so weak, so feeble. Nevertheless, every year the principal lowered his head, entered the inhospitable terrain in the halls of the Leaksville Board of Education, and begged for his students - yet again.

The Professor's close friends and family thought Bill O. Wright's Booker T. Washington style of leadership was not beneficial to the *Negro Cause*, and they told him so; even though everyone had to admit that he did manage to get a lot of supplies for the Douglas School. But, how much should that count if the supplies he acquired were White folk's cast-offs? Still, Professor Wright thought of Booker T. Washington as his role model; he admired the fact that Booker T. was a man who did whatever he had to do to get the necessary supplies for his people. Booker T. persuaded White businessmen to make substantial contributions to his school, and still coped with the criticism he got from other leaders in the Black community. It was a tightrope the Professor hoped he could manage to walk. He was trying.

Bill O. Wright researched and studied as much as he could about this great educator, the founder of Tuskegee Institute; in fact, he learned that the 'T' in the educator's name stood for 'Taliaferro'. The Professor had a friend in Hampton, Va. whose last name was Taliaferro; he wondered if it was possible that his friend might be related to Booker T. Washington. He liked to think that was a real possibility because Booker T. went to Hampton Institute.

Sometimes after a meeting with the Board of Ed. Professor Bill O. Wright felt the twinge of a chest pain, or a stomach cramp. When he looked out of his window and watched the neighbors drift to the home of Mr. and Mrs. Keys, the Professor wondered if anyone appreciated, or even knew, what he was going through for their children. Then he reprimanded himself for that thought... It didn't matter what he thought; the only thing that mattered was what he did - what he was able to accomplish. The Professor vowed to do everything he could in his lifetime to leave this world a better place for his people; he lived with acceptance of the loneliness which accompanied his self determined mission... As Professor Bill O. Wright sat quietly at his desk, he looked intently at the large picture of Booker T. Washington that hung on the opposite wall.

The old folks said: *"He who learns but does not think is lost, and he who thinks but does not learn is in great danger.*

SNAKES

Ed drove pass a crumbling red brick chimney standing alone in a flat yellow, plumb, burgundy, green and white yard - an explosion of wild flowers, amid a weed infestation. The pseudo-brick shingled house that used to be there has been gone for several years; when it burned down, the intense fire could be seen miles away. Ed recalled a statement he once heard but can't remember where… *'Weeds are just plants growing in the wrong place, so if you enjoy the plants that appear, just leave them. Wild flowers are delightful splashes of color with which Mother Nature adorns her landscape.'*

Ed rationalized as he fought back an insurmountable wave of sadness… So nature was compensating with things of beauty to cover up where ugliness occurred. There was supposed to be a home there!

The evening of the fire Ed knew something terrible had happened on his route because of the bellowing smoke he saw on the horizon as he relaxed with his wife on the comfortable glider on his front porch, miles away from the source. Suellen noticed it first, she thought it was an odd colored cloud formation; then, they both quickly realized it was really smoke against the early evening sky, and it was coming from the vicinity of Price Road. Ed and Suellen jumped into their car and rode out to Price Road to see exactly what was burning.

Ed's heart felt as if it gave away its designated space within his body and actually fell - somewhere around his stomach, when he saw the devastation. It happened years ago, yet Ed still couldn't drive pass the desolate chimney without recalling the same all-consuming air he inhaled that night - albeit fleeting. When Ed and Suellen arrived at the scene, the night it happened, they found themselves the only White people there.

Uncle Dada, his wife, and children were all huddled together surrounded by concerned friends and family. It appeared that all the Colored people who lived on Price Road were standing nearby watching the last embers glow as the night sky cast a dark blanket over the land.

Ed approached Lyndell and Zara; they were standing near Delphine and her father, Deacon Riley. Ed held Suellen's hand; he knew she might feel uncomfortable because she really didn't know everybody as he did. He talked to her about the people he met on his route when he got home everyday, so Suellen knew the names; however, the night of the fire was the first time Ed brought Suellen to Price Road.

"What on God's earth happened?" Ed asked into the group, as he tucked his wife's hand under his arm pulling her close to his side. It was Uncle DaDa Ashford's home that was ablaze. "They set fire to da house." Deacon Riley answered Ed's question as they stood together that night with a resigned *'oh well'* sound in his deflated voice.

"Who did it?" Ed quizzed Deacon Riley hesitantly while his gut told him not to ask the question at all. Deacon Riley turned slightly toward Ed and whispered,

"They came from town... Slithered in like snakes on horseback, through the growth back there." Deacon Riley nodded his head slightly toward the thicket of trees, flames created an eerie reflection on the leaves and branches. Ed blinked his eyes; with the back of his hand he tried to wipe away the sight of his disbelief, for he thought he saw a shadowy image of a woman sitting very still and erect on horseback... Lilith?

Ed's attention was yanked back as he became aware that the Deacon was continuing to speak. Ed involuntarily inhaled; the air did not seem to want to leave his chest. He blinked again; the smell of the burning house reminded him of charcoal on the grill at a picnic. In the haze of the smoke filled air, finally, Ed exhaled as he turned to look directly at the Deacon... Deacon Riley' stood like a wilted statue, his lips hardly moved - his words forced to escape from the confinement of his new upper and lower dental plates; in fact, he never even looked in Ed's direction.

"The low down snakes slinked back that way too... Didn't no-body see no faces."

From town... That was Deacon Riley's way of letting Ed know that the fire was started by White people. Ed understood... A few years earlier, before he became a mailman on Price Road, that kind of insinuation would have escaped his comprehension. An involuntary grunt escaped from Ed's oral cavity and was lost in the mesh of smoke and embers. He slowly turned around, and lead the way back to his car.

There was nothing Ed could do; furthermore, they were the only White people at the scene... He felt it was best for them to leave. He restrained himself from running, screaming, yelling... In spite of all the things Ed's innards wanted to do he managed to contain himself and walked, almost zombie-like, to his car. Ed and Suellen did not have a discussion about anything on the way home. There was a silence that hung heavy within the circumference of the car that night.

There was so much going through Ed's head... He had never shared his inner feelings with his wife: his own confounded thoughts about the Colored and White conflict, his absolute confusion about the United States Government's segregation laws, the Christian Church's role in slavery, the legality of Jim Crow, and the hatred that exhibited itself in primeval acts such as the fire. He needed to talk to someone, but he sat in silence... Ed was apprehensive about having that discussion with Suellen; he was agonized by his uncertainty of how his wife felt. He didn't want to spoil their relationship. Conflicting views might emerge like a worm in an apple; that image scared him, besides he was still trying to discover his own viewpoint of these issues. So, he kept all his feelings to himself.

* * *

Mr. Ashford was a Saponi Indian who was married to Ornella, a Colored woman, for over forty-five years. Everybody, children and adults alike, called this congenial man Uncle DaDa although he didn't have any natural nieces or nephews.

"DaDa," his oldest child, Daisy, squealed. Her first words were without a doubt meant for the six foot tall man, with a very muscular build, who made her laugh as he held her high toward the sky. From that position, baby Daisy looked down into her father's penetrating eyes, supported by high cheek bones and a strong jaw line while she alternately dribbled and shrieked... "DaDa, DaDa." Everybody in the community followed Daisy's lead, and Mr. Ashford became DaDa. The 'Uncle' part was added by children who recognized that he was not their father, but they still wanted to feel related to him in some way.

Uncle DaDa's own children, three boys and four girls, were repeatedly told by their playmates that they had the best father in the world. Many of the children along Price Road wished their own fathers were more like Uncle DaDa.

Uncle DaDa usually wore a wide brimmed natural straw hat adorned, on the left side, with a plume of brightly colored feathers tucked into a carved dark brown leather headband. Uncle DaDa always warned the children to wear a hat so they would not have a sun stroke; consequently, almost all of the children on Price Road owned a smaller version of DaDa's straw hat – a gift from him.

As he aged, Uncle DaDa did less and less farm work, but he was constantly busy working on some hand made project - gifts for his own grandchildren and the neighborhood children. When the gift was finished, Uncle DaDa would gather his young crowd together for an impromptu presentation. There would always be a valid reason for the chosen one to receive the gift at that time.

Uncle DaDa always stood in the middle of his porch - high above the small group of children on his front yard. The excitement of the children carried over to the adults; therefore, many of the parents walked over to the Ashford home to be part of the fun. Uncle DaDa always started his little ceremony by saying, "You children know I have eyes 'n da back of ma head, and I'm always watching ta see how you're behaving. Today I want ta compliment a couple of people on what I believe is real good behavior, the kind that deserves a reward." In reality the parents secretly told Uncle DaDa, when their children did good deeds, and the children were never sure of how Uncle DaDa seemed to know so much about them.

One day when the neighbors gathered in his yard, Uncle DaDa held up a hand made beaded leather pouch and a newly made straw hat.

"I have noticed you, Mark. You have been a good big brother ta your sister. I saw you help her get up when she fell, 'n you brushed the dirt off a her knee. You showed her the concern dat a big brother cares... You were kind ta your sister; therefore Mark, you deserve a 'Good Big Brother' reward for dat. OK, come 'n get it!" Uncle DaDa said.

Little seven year old Mark's look of surprise gave way to a wide grin when he heard his name. Mark's eyes avoided everything and everyone except the ground in front of him; he walked slowly, and deliberately, with his head bowed as he climbed the four steps up to the porch. Uncle DaDa handed Mark the pouch while the group applauded. Mark couldn't stop smiling. He jumped off the porch and ran into his mother's arms hugging onto his reward.

"Now, just one mo' gift today. Mary, will you please come ta get dis hat, it's yours. I saw your mother working hard last Monday, doing the laundry, 'n you were working hard right b'side her. You were'nt pouting 'n fussing 'bout hav'ng ta help, I noticed how much of'a help you were ta yo'r mom, and ya didn't even know dat I saw you. Did you?" Uncle DaDa teased as he handed eight year old Mary the straw hat, with a twinkle in his eye. Mary was so happy, she took the fancy straw hat, with a deep 'thank you' curtsey, and put it on immediately. She could hardly stop jumping up and down while everybody gave her hugs of congratulations.

After everybody calmed down, Mary said to Uncle DaDa, "Please tell us some more 'bout yo'r life! Please! Please," she begged, leading the group in a chant, "Please Uncle DaDa tell us a story! Please tell us a story!"

"OK, calm down and I will tell you an interesting story about my people," said DaDa, giving in to the request as usual.

"Well, as you know, I am a Saponi Indian. There were only twenty people 'n my tribe when I was born; but we're part of the larger Saponi Nation. Most of my people are from North Carolina and Virginia." said Uncle DaDa as he began his familiar saga.

"My ancestors, who lived here 'fore da time of George Washington's birth, were forced ta live on the *Fort Christanna Reservation* in Brunswick County, VA. That was a place that the Governor of Virginia built ta confine de Indians together on da East Coast." Uncle DaDa said.

"That was 'fore they made ma people walk de Trail Of Tears... Forced all of the Indians they could round up to go out West, ta live on the Reservations." Uncle DaDa ignored the raised hands in the crowd as he continued his saga.

"Anyway, that's another story… The Indians were told that Fort Christanna was named for *Christ* and *Queen Anne*. It always amazed me that the Fort was named fo' Christ when it was not a Christ-like place at all, but I guess it was 'pposed to make the Indians feel better if they were told that both Christ 'n the Queen were involved in such a horrible place." Uncle DaDa commented.

"The Indians, who were herded into the Fort, came from several different tribes from all over North Carolina and Virginia. They basically spoke da same language. The College of William and Mary ran a school at da fort; their students would come ta teach basic English. Now… the real reason for de Fort was ta keep de Indians separate from da Colored slaves." Uncle DaDa continued.

"Why did they want ta keep da Indians and da Colored people apart?" questioned a voice from the group.

"Well, they realized that de Indians 'n the Negro races possess'd similar talents. The White captors were afraid if'n the two groups ever pooled their resources 'n knowledge that there would be an uprising they wouldn't be able ta handle." Uncle DaDa said. "The White folks was scared they would be outnumbered in this 'New World' they *discovered*, so it was a way to make sure the slave owners stayed in control; dey tried ta keep everybody on lockdown. " he explained.

"Then what happened Uncle DaDa?" an anxious child's voice called out.

"You know how White folks have a hard time telling a Colored person from an Indian 'cause the races favor each other. Both of us come in so many shades; in fact, when an Indian stands beside a Negro the White man usually can't tell which is which. You know how there are some Negroes who can pass for White; well, there are some Indians that passed for Negro, and other Indians that can pass for White." Uncle Dada said.

"Indians did whatever they had to do to stay near their homeland. So my great - great – great - grandfather was able to hide with a Free Negro family when Fort Christanna was closed in 1720. All he had ta do was to pretend ta be a member of da Colored family; that's why I live here – my ancestor didn't get marched off ta de Reservation. He was dark skinned, and he blended in with de Colored people; it t'was a choice he made, not that he had much ta choose from – sort of like choosing between de Devil 'n da deep blue sea. Golden Arrow - dat was his name - knew of other Indians who also hid wid da families of slaves or freemen. Others were light enough ta pass fo' White and pretended to be White travelers – nomads - not spending too much time 'n one place, whereas de White people never suspected. The Indians would know each other's secret, but they never betrayed each other.

Ma Paw told us 'bout members of de same tribe who might pass each other on de road; one, who looked White, might be walking free wid his White friends whilst the other, who was darker, was a slave. The two could pass each other without anyone realizing that they even knew each other. They might be brothers or sisters, maybe even mother or father and child; still, except for a special exchange of glances – a silent communication sent by the eyes or a head motion of the connector that was only understood by the connectee, no one would never even guess that such outwardly dissimilar souls knew each other at all. Oh, they had ta be clever; it t'was a matter of life or death." DaDa said.

Uncle DaDa had to leave some of the information out of his story, or he would be talking all night. Just the techniques the Indians used for survival in such a racially hostile climate were fascinating stories that could be told at other times.

"Golden Arrow t'was a farmer as were all the male children 'n his line of descent; therefore, ma Paw, 'n his father, 'n I were farmers. It was through this birth line dat knowledge of de land came down ta me 'n ma children, 'n that's what I teach ta you that are willing to learn." Uncle DaDa was proud to know and share the history of his family line; he was aware that most of his friends, the Negro families along Price Road, could only trace their family tree for one or possibly two generations.

"I learned how to burn the fields to prepare for planting." he continued.

"Did you know the Saponi Indians are also known as de Blackfoot Indians? That's 'cause of de black ash that got on our feet when we walked through de brush dat we burned in the field." Uncle DaDa explained.

The children were wide-eyed; they bubbled with questions. They loved to hear Uncle DaDa's stories. The children's excitement was begging to be satisfied, even if it was a story they had heard twenty-thousand times before. Sometimes Uncle Dada included his uncle, Mr. Sycamore, in the recounting of their tribal history. The way Uncle DaDa told a story was almost like a one man stage show; he was extremely dramatic in the presentation of each episode. His voice extended into crescendos, and his body arranged itself in formations to increase the punctuation of every concept; sometimes he banged on a near-by object such as a chair, table, or a pillar on the porch to make the sound of a drum as an accessory to the story. Most times the children artfully extended the narrative by asking questions for which they already knew the answer.

"Uncle DaDa, why did ya'll burn the fields?"

Then, he would answer patiently - with a dramatic touch, "Well, it cleared da ground 'n made it more fertile so things would grow better. We had ta be careful not ta let the fire burn more than we wanted it to. Ma father taught me how ta control the fire. Fire is one of the most useful things man has discovered, but it can be one of de most dangerous if it's not controlled." he told them.

Uncle DaDa always took time to warn the children of the dangers of uncontrolled fire. He sometimes took the time to show them how to make fire with a flint, a kind of stone that Indians used to create a spark.

Sometimes there were cookouts around the special circular pit Uncle DaDa made from the strategic placement of large stones; family and friends sat around the pit to roast marshmallows and tell stories on holidays. They placed potatoes, yams, and whole ears of corn - still wrapped in its husk, on the charcoals to cook; after which, Uncle DaDa and Mr. Sycamore gave lessons on how to make smoke signals.

"So, people began ta call us Blackfoot; the name stuck so much that very few people know that we're really Saponi Indians." Uncle DaDa continued, holding his foot up high for all to see. He really was a beautiful caramel color; however, if Uncle DaDa said his foot was black no-one was going to question it.

As he looked over the small audience in his yard, he saw his friends, people that were young and not as young; many of them were holding treasures they received from Uncle DaDa in a similar ceremony in past years. DaDa's wife, Ornella, and their children helped throughout the years to make a wide assortment of interesting treasures to give away such as: dried apple dolls [face features were molded onto a dried apple], corn husk dolls [bodies were made from corn husk with hair made from the silk-like top on an ear of corn], carved wooden nick-knacks [such as horses, rabbits, pigs, etc], pick- up-sticks, woven baskets of various shapes, leather pouches, wallets, hand and shoulder bags, book covers, book markers, and woven belts. It was a continuous project that the entire Ashford family enjoyed working on together.

Some nights Uncle DaDa walked around his yard, or sat on his porch in a solitary vigil – looking for signs of a snake. Whenever DaDa discovered a swirl in the dirt, the footprint of a passing snake, he tracked the snake and terminated its vile existence.

The old folks at the store laughingly teased Uncle DaDa, "Man… you have every snake in de county 'fraid ta come onto yo'r property. Word is out, in 'Snakeville,' that any snake found on Uncle DaDa's land might end up as a snakeskin belt or as da top of a pair of sandals" they said.

Almost everybody on Price Road, at one time or other, received a special handcrafted gift - a special reward from Uncle DaDa Ashford's family..

The church ladies put their hands together and sang, "*This little light of mine, I'm going to let it shine.*"

And, almost all the snakes stayed away from Uncle DaDa's house… **Then, there was the fire…** Ed thought… Some snakes got onto Uncle DaDa's property that night. Someone ought to be skinned alive for that dastardly deed! Ed wished he had the nerve to do something with the information he had because he knew who the snakes were… When Suellen woke him up last night, she said, "What's the matter Ed? Did you have another bad dream?" Years had passed since the fire, yet Ed still had nights of restless sleep.

The old folks said… *Belief determines values – values determine behavior.*

FEED, SEED, AND ALL YOU NEED

As Ed continued down Price Road, he approached the McNeal's general store. Ed found a parking space in front of the store while he looked to see if the usual hang-a-round-quartet of friends were sitting on the low, one-step-up porch… If the old folks were not there, something was wrong… The original hand painted sign hung over the front porch of the store; it announced boldly for all to see, **FEED, SEED, AND ALL YOU NEED!** Bags of cattle feed were represented, on the sign, by clumsy amateur artwork.

The family owned store was owned by Mo McNeal and his wife Lily. Mo's grandfather opened the store about ten years after the Emancipation Proclamation as a supply post for the surrounding share-croppers. When Mo and Lily, took over the store, they expanded the services the country store offered. The McNeil family never did socialize very much with the townspeople; they had their own little close-knit world right there on Price Road, and their family members never felt the need to be 'accepted' by anyone in particular.

The McNeil's two grown boys, P.C. and L.V., chose to use initials rather than their given names when they started school. At an early age, both boys questioned their parent's choice of baby names. P.C. was the McNeil's oldest child.

"You were such a perfect child – that's why we named you '*Perfect Child.*' We thought the name fit you just right." Mo and Lily told the one who preferred to be known as P.C.

"You have a birthmark that looks like a leaf on your shoulder; we imagined that God marked you special 'cause he loves you so much. We love you too, so that's why we gave you the name '*Leaf Venus.*'" Mo and Lily told their youngest child, the one who called himself L.V.

P.C. and L.V. operated the outdoor mechanic shop/ auto grave yard on the side of the store; they worked under a wide extended green tin carport that was surrounded by an abundance of auto skeletons and carcasses. Both P.C and L.V. loved to tinker with cars; neither man was a great mechanic, but they could help customers in case of an emergency - such as a flat tire or dead battery. Whenever a gas customer drove up, the aspiring mechanics stopped whatever work they were doing on a car to pump the Texaco gas. It was beneficial to the travelers along Price Road that the Mc Neal's family store, fifteen miles from town, was almost a complete service station. Most times all the McNeil family members worked together without a problem, but there were those times when communication niceties faltered; then, it was pure comic entertainment to hear the family lay each other out.

The McNeils all lived together in the three bedroom house that was an extension to the back of the store. The house was not well kept; Lily spent most of her day working in the store, she was not going to clean up after three grown men at the end of the day; consequently, the house had not really been thoroughly cleaned in years.

When she couldn't stand the disarray any longer, Lily found something to do in the store. Sometimes, to keep her rage contained, she walked down the road to visit with a neighbor. Lily was determined that she was not going to allow the men-folk to assume that because she was a woman she alone was responsible for all the housework. Lily reached the point that she kept the boy's bedroom doors closed, so she couldn't see the mess. The clutter and disorder in their rooms was the image of the aftermath of a hurricane, it gave Lily a headache…

P.C. was very outgoing, his personality was smooth and debonair; he was tall and thin, yet muscular, with a full head of blond hair. Young ladies often drove out from town to get gas as an excuse to say hello to P.C. and look into his blue eyes. He didn't notice that he was the rooster in the hen house. P.C. was much more interested in cars. Although the ladies loved him, P.C. sometimes honestly forgot a date because he was working on a car. P.C. hated to have serious disturbances among family and friends, and he would do whatever he could to bring resolutions to any conflicts. His family and friends considered P.C. as a peacemaker; they often sought him out in the same way that one would go to a judge - to have him solve a dispute.

L.V. was slightly shorter than his brother, and a miniature image of his father. Since L.V. was more of an introvert than his brother, he was very seldom in the center of a conversation. He was more likely to be found standing off to the side, listening to others talk, unless the conversations were about car races. L.V. went to the Danville, VA, or the Highpoint, NC. Speedway, every time there was a race; that could be every weekend depending on the season of the year. L.V. was the dependable foundation of the family; he was always there to help anybody whenever he could as long as he could schedule things not to interfere with his beloved car races.

* * *

When Perry and Illanna's oldest son, Weldon, came to take Illanna and Iris for their visit to Baltimore (in1949), he drove to the McNeil's store to gas up for the trip. Both P.C and L.V. walked around Weldon's shinny new Black '49 Ford, with the leather seats; their twenty fingers touched the glistening hood of the car carefully, ever so lightly… Weldon just stood by and watched, his chest poked out as P.C. and L.V.'s eyes caressed every aspect of his car's design. P.C. and L.V. examined the car, from the front grill to the back bumper, and talked to Weldon Wheatly about its capabilities. It was a conversation of mutual respect… All three shared a mutual interest - cars.

"How does this baby handle?" asked P.C.

"Handles like a dream, lightweight - only weigh 'bout two hundr'd 'n tw'ny lbs. That's less than de 1948 model. It's easier ta steer than de older models, 'n gives great gas mileage… Didn't even use a whole tank of gas ta come down here from Baltimore." Weldon answered.

"How she ride?" asked L.V.

"She rides like you sitting on a sofa 'n de living room. It's that kind of comfort… I'm telling ya it's like you cruising, even 'n the back seat!" Weldon said as he pretended to steer - bending at the knees to give the effect of sitting behind the wheel.

"Let's take a short ride up da road." P.C. suggested.

"Sure, come on… I'll ride you up to the road bend 'n front of Mrs. Freesia Holly's house, I've got ta get back 'fore Big Mom wonder where I am." Weldon offered.

Meanwhile, Illanna thought she was going to have a heart attack from worry. Illanna couldn't imagine what was keeping her son at the store for so long. She tried not to worry unnecessarily, but when Colored people didn't show up within a reasonable time a mother was going to worry. When her son finally returned, safe and unharmed, Illanna was relieved; nevertheless, she couldn't resist giving Weldon, who towered over her, a pretend spanking. Weldon danced around the kitchen before he caught his mother in an affectionate bear hug.

It was also the day that the three young men, two white and one black, developed a friendship based on an automotive love affair - despite old Mr. Jim Crow. The McNeal store was a staple ingredient on Price Road... Interesting friendships seemed to develop, grow, and persevere in the relaxed retail atmosphere.

The old folks said... *It takes a minute to find a special friend, an hour to appreciate them; then, you'll never forget them.*

MEADOW WOODS

Ed pinched his lips together, in determination not to be so sentimental on his last day as the mailman on the route, when he said goodbye to the group on the porch. Ed continued to drive down the road; he passed Meadow Woods, a nightclub located near the end of Price Road as it approached the rural extension of Stoneville. Ed was always intrigued by the club's owner, Mr. Udell's son, Tyree - a handsome, middle aged, world traveler. Ed stopped at Tyree Udell's mailbox. Tyree lived alone in a small brick house on the grassy knoll next to his nightclub. He was not married, and an abundance of ladies tried to woo Tyree Udell with: good home baking, good treatment [cleaning his house, washing and ironing his clothes, etc.], and good loving… Tyree used his natural charm to seduce one lady after the other. Tyree was single, but he was hardly ever without female companionship.

Tyree Udell played a little piano and a lot of trumpet; he traveled on tour buses with jazz bands all over the United States in the late 30s and early 1940s. He never took the time to cultivate a love relationship; music was his first love. Whenever one band collapsed Tyree joined another. He paid his dues by playing for years on what entertainers referred to as *'The Chicken Bone Circuit'*. In better days Tyree Udell played with some of the best musicians in the industry.

Tyree was playing with Cab Calloway's band in 1941 when Cab Calloway and Dizzy Gillespie actually got into a fight precipitated by a spitball Dizzy threw at Cab. Dizzy was playful, and he often amused himself at Cab's expense; the spitball incident was just one time too many – the last straw for Cab. Tyree always believed it was just a personality clash between Calloway and Dizzy, so he tried to be a peacemaker - to get the two great talents to continue to work together; however, it would be years before Cab Calloway and Dizzy Gillespie even spoke to each other again.

After the spitball incident, Dizzy left Cab's band; Tyree followed. Both of them joined a brand new group started by their mutual friend,

Charlie Parker; they had all played together with Earl [Fatha] Hines' band in Chicago at one time. When 'Fatha' hired Billy Eckstine as the band vocalist, Billy and Tyree became good friends. The two men respected each other; they spent many after-hours together as they drank, jammed, and shared life stories. Billy told Tyree, as they shared a pint of whiskey after a club engagement, about his decision to change the spelling of his name.

"I changed the spelling from Eckstein to Eckstine because I was running into problems... Billy said. "Man, everybody thought I was Jewish before they even saw me. Well, that was more trouble than it was worth. So man, I fixed that problem - just changed the spelling... I got enough problems being Colored; don't need to add nothing to that." Billy added as he emptied his shot-glass in one gulp, and rocked back on the rear legs of his chair.

Tyree always thought Billy Eckstine was a competent trumpet player, but he thought Billy was a better singer. The two friends were sometimes brutally blunt - but always straight up honest with each other.

"Man you can blow alright, but God gave you some real pipes... That's your natural instrument! Leave the horn to me." Tyree told Billy.

Tyree always felt it was his influence that inspired Billy Eckstine to form his own band in 1943, and to market the fashion line of Billy Eckstine signature shirts and string necktie sets.

"The people love you man... 'specially the ladies... might as well use your Mo-Jo to your advantage." Tyree said to Billy. Not long after that conversation Tyree left Charlie Parker's band to go on the road with Eckstine.

Tyree spent his money as fast as he made it; therefore, when he had a stroke, it was Billy Eckstine who paid for Tyree's medical bills and train ticket home - to North Carolina... If you didn't know, you couldn't discern that Tyree had experienced a stroke; it didn't do a lot of damage, but it forced him to leave the road tour. Leaksville, NC was 'home' for Tyree, so he came back to recuperate where he grew up and had family and friends - back to Price Road.

Tyree's parents convinced him to stay home. His father, Mr. Udell, kept his friends at the McNeal general store, updated about his son's health. Everybody said, "We are praying for Tyree." The entire population of Price Road was proud of what this home-grown son had accomplished; in fact, many of the local residents lived vicariously through Tyree's experiences. The stories he told held everybody captivated, including Ed. It was nice having Tyree back home. It was like having a celebrity around, but most of all they were concerned about Tyree's health and well being. Tyree finally submitted to his family's appeal for him not to return to playing on the road, a lifestyle that seemed to be slowly killing him.

Tyree had to admit that leaving the road travel was a good thing for him, but he still missed the nightlife; therefore, he opened the nightclub he named 'Meadow Woods'. Tyree Udell knew what a sophisticated nightclub business should look like since he had spent so much time in nightspots in: Harlem, Chicago, small towns, and big towns. Tyree was confident that he could recreate the same big city atmosphere in Leaksville's rural community.

The empty building Tyree found was originally The Meadow Greens Country Club until the 'White Only' membership built new accommodations at a new location. The white washed log cabin facility, with green trim, was accessible from Price Road; Tyree thought it was the perfect space for a swanky nightclub which would attract the more progressive Negro, a different clientele than Hilltop and Black Bottom served. Everybody in Tyree's family pitched in to decorate the building according to his visualization… His dream…

It was a simple design; the party atmosphere was created with mirrors, lights, and colorful tablecloths. There was a jukebox with: red, blue, and yellow lights, and most of the current 45's. On some nights a live house band played under Tyree's direction. The group was a composite of aspiring young local musicians who played every thing they could find including tin tubs and washboards - all of them in hopes of a musical ticket off the farm - maybe to follow in Tyree's footsteps. He was a role model - whether he wanted to be or not.

Tyree sometimes played and sang, with a little nudge. It didn't take much to persuade Tyree to perform, he loved the applause. However, Tyree was happiest whenever an old road-buddy stopped to visit; when that happened, Tyree's personality exploded. Eventually the word spread throughout the music industry, up and down the East coast, "Tyree Udell owns the Meadow Woods Night Club, on Price Road, outside Leaksville, NC." Whenever a road trip brought any of those old friends close to Leaksville, Tyree got a surprise visit. That was when an impromptu jazz session replaced verbal conversation. The music was a beautiful level of communication, for the musicians, since it allowed the expression of inner feelings not easily stated in any other way.

"Man I'm glad you are doing well," said the trumpet - setting the pitch.

"You really look good man. Life must be treating you swell." improvised the piano keys in arpeggio.

"So, how long can you stay?" asked the percussions.

"Not long, I have to leave today." answered the bass in true cadenza showmanship… The audience applauded, and the beat went on…

Sarah Vaughan, Charlie Parker, Earl 'Fatha' Hines, and Lionel Hampton have all visited the Meadow Woods Nightclub at least one time. Ed heard about an unbelievable tenor saxophone 'battle' one Saturday night when Dexter Gordon and Wardell Gray faced off at Meadow Woods. Someone had to explain to Ed that the 'battle' was not a physical fight. It took Ed a little time to understand the fact that friends competed in friendly musical excursions, and called it a battle; it was a concept that Tyree called "Copesetic."

The residents of Price Road were still laughing and talking about another visitor for years after the Meadow Woods event. Count Basie stopped to visit Tyree. Basie and his singer, Joe Williams, were on their way to back to Harlem. Tyree Udell didn't know Joe personally, but he and Basie went 'way back'; they were 'cut buddies' in the old days. Even people who never went to a nightclub were sorry they missed that impromptu session; Joe's butter-silk voice, Basie on the piano, and Tyree on the trumpet, it was a feel-good-partying-good-time. They jammed all night.

Nineteen year old Myron Flowers, who was a relative of Ed's veteran friend Nardu Hearst, had never been inside the Meadow Woods Nightclub. Myron was born and raised in 'Black Bottom'. When he heard about Count Basie's visit, the shy young man dressed in the best outfit he could put together with the help of his relatives in Black Bottom. In spite of the tight ball of nerves gathered in his stomach, Myron went to Meadow Woods with his clarinet tucked firmly under his arm.

"C-C-Can I sit in with y-y-you?" Myron stammered nervously. Hardly anyone heard him. Tyree recognized Myron as a resident of the Price Road community; he remembered hearing that the young man had some musical ability. Tyree, in the mood of a benevolent friend, wrapped his arm around Myron's shoulder and ushered him onto the small platform that served as a stage. The atmosphere in the room was harmonious, encouraged by the melodic flow of sweet sounds and whiskey.

Myron, hesitant at first, slowly began to contribute to the rhythm. Count Basie's head, turned slightly to the side, bobbed to the beat as his fingers caressed the piano keys; his eyebrows stretched toward his hairline while Myron's clarinet modulated in a delightful union.

"Man you can really play." The Count said to Myron. It was a statement of fact and surprise. When Basie asked Myron if he wanted to go on to New York with them, it was Myron's turn to be surprised - although it was his dream come true. Myron didn't waste any time running home to pack... He left with Basie and Joe the next morning; it was a Sunday, the beginning of a new week – and the beginning of a new life for Myron. The entire neighborhood was talking...

"Did ya hear da latest news? Myron Flowers, from Black Bottom done gone ta New York with Count Basie 'n Joe Williams."

"He never had no lessons, just natural talent."

"His momma say Nardu gave him the clarinet when he was little, been play'ng ever since."

It was the chatter up and down Price Road. This music thing was working for someone, everybody was inspired! Myron was the talk of the town. Nardu's chest swelled with enormous pride; he did not know when he gave the clarinet to Myron that it was a key to a future for the boy.

"Found it in the trash dump, brought it home 'n cleaned and shined it; it just needed a new mouth piece. I gave it ta Myron; he's one child who always loved music... Didn't have no idea he would do what he did wid'it...Yes sir I'm proud of him!" Nardu told Ed.

* * *

Since Ed had never been inside the Meadow Woods Club, he was very curious; it appeared to him that all entering those doors could count on having fun. The laughter, music, and songs filtered out of the windows and doors; the full notes floated to the treetops where they hung, wailing, waiting to be heard, without apology, throughout the woods and farmlands on Price Road.

That was part of Ed's amazement about Negroes. They always seemed to have fun, in spite of the problems and troubles he knew they had. And, Ed really did know a lot about the personal affairs of the people on his route. He delivered their mail, and he didn't want to call himself nosey; he thought of himself as observant.

Every Monday morning Ed overheard conversations among the residents along Price Road as he delivered the mail. He watched; he listened; he took notice - sometimes in awe, to the conversations – the re-telling, the various - sometimes melodramatic descriptions of the activities of the previous weekend. Sometimes, in their excitement, the Meadow Woods patrons would share stories of their experiences directly with Ed. Those Monday morning exchanges made the day worth looking forward to. Ed felt like he was on a scavenger hunt where the most exciting tid-bit of information might be found anyplace: sometimes at the McNeil store, sometimes a gathering at a mailbox. Ed consciously tried to ask questions of the story tellers in a friendly non-judgmental way, and he learned so much.

Most of all Ed learned to stop being so self conscious. He learned that Colored people accepted him best when he allowed the *Inner Ed* to come through without editing. He learned that Colored people didn't seem to respond as well to his *Outer Ed* persona. Within a few years, Ed had reached the point when he considered the people on his route as his friends... But, a thought resonated in Ed's brain... Could he honestly say they were his friends? Was a person really considered as a friend if they never associated outside of his work?

When Ed tried to analyze his inner feelings about this notion, he experienced a sensation he found hard to understand. It felt a little like envy... Could that be a truth? He wondered... Ed struggled with emotions deep inside his level of comprehension... Was it possible that he felt a longing to understand what seemed to be the Negroes' ability to put bona fide troubles aside, and genuinely enjoy life, for at least a few hours each weekend because **he** wished for that ability? How was it that hope always seemed to be alive through desperate times? Was the ability to laugh at misery, to sing in the face of pain - and call it the Blues, Jazz, or Soul the Negro people's prescription for survival? Ed had so many questions...

The old folks said... *Even in laughter the heart is sorrowful; and the end of that mirth is heaviness.* Proverbs 14:13

ONE DROP?

Ed was a people watcher...

Ed observed and He remembered the talk, action, and reaction among his family and friends when only White people were around – when there was the atmosphere of a White folk's inner sanctum. White folks talked about Colored folks in their segregated barber shops, churches, and even over evening dinner in their homes; wherever White folks gathered the subject would almost certainly come up. During his lifetime Ed overheard so many conversations about 'those Niggras,' and Ed listened...

Ed was a good listener...

He paid close attention to everybody. In fact, sometimes his listening made him more confused than anything because Ed heard so many contradictory statements from White people. For example, Ed heard many White people say, "That Niggra, Jackie Robinson, ain't got no business playing with the Dodgers." Ed observed the people who jeered when Robinson stepped up to bat, yet they were the same people who cheered when the Dodgers won a game. Ed heard White people admit that Joe Louis, the Brown Bomber, was a great boxer while they got really emotionally involved in a prayer to God to let a White boxer (a Great White Hope) "beat the snot outta that upstart Niggra;" nevertheless, the same people prayed for Joe Louis to win whenever he represented the United States. White people loved *Gone With The Wind* because of the movie's charming southern intonation, yet they were incensed at Hollywood for acknowledging Hattie McDaniel with an Oscar for the best supporting actress. They loved to hear Nat 'King' Cole sing, but they only wanted to listen to his music - not see him; hence, Nat Cole was not welcomed to buy a house in a White neighborhood. In fact, it was difficult to find a sponsor for Nat 'King' Cole to host a television show because White people vowed to boycott the advertised product. Ed observed White people as they purchased suntan lotion, specifically to add more color to their skin; however, at the same time, those same White people regarded all Colored people as subordinate - like any beast of burden - just because of their darker skin color.

Ed was a logical thinker...

Ed realized that all White folks did not feel that way, but he only heard the ones talk who did. Ed thought... There must be others, like him, who disagreed with the loud mouth agitators. But, where were they? Sometimes Ed felt he was hiding behind a hollow sentiment... Were his opinions, his thoughts, enclosed in silence because he was actually afraid? He wondered if other White people remained silent during these vile opinionated conversations, like he did, for the same reason.

He thought about something called the *one drop rule,* which was a concept he was taught by all the adults around him as a truth. The *one drop rule* stated - if there was a Negro ancestor, anywhere on the family tree, it was the one drop that was enough to deem all of the descendants in that bloodline a Negro. Because Ed saw Colored people whose skin was lighter than some White people, and some White people who had Negroid features, he questioned the logic of the one drop rule... How could *anyone* be sure of their racial heritage? When Ed thought about all of this, he was befuddled.

Ed wondered...

He wondered if it were possible for people, who considered themselves as White, to have Colored blood in their family tree that they didn't personally know about? Then, his logic answered the question from the small voice in his head. Ed tried not to wallow in those thoughts; his head felt heavy - as if his thoughts had overloaded his senses. Ed reasoned to himself... *Of course it was possible!*

Ed continued to develop the concept of racial impurity in his analytical mode... Nobody knew the heritage of *all* of their ancestors; one only knew whatever they were told by their relatives, which may or may not be true. Ed's brow wrinkled with the depth of his thinking; it was enough to give him a low grade ache at his forehead... Still, Ed couldn't stop the thoughts; it was hard to turn his brain off - even when he tried to sleep.

He thought about the fact that there were Colored people who could pass for White, without being detected. One only had to look around them and they would see many Colored people who fulfilled the White person's visual description. Ed imagined how a person, who was raised to believe they were White – taught all the prejudices, would react if it came to light that they had a Colored ancestor? What would that knowledge do? Would it suddenly convert them into a Colored person according to the One Drop Rule? Would they be forced by their previous friends and acquaintances to live under the existing laws of Jim Crow segregation? What about their children? If their White-looking children moved away from the people who knew them, would they - could they become White again?

Ed talked to himself...

Sometimes Ed actually talked to himself while he delivered the mail. "Would knowing that there was Colored blood make a person different? Would that person suddenly become less human? Did it only matter if somebody knew? Was the obvious physical difference of color between the Negro and the Caucasian the only reason this segregation thing worked?" Ed pondered out loud to the emptiness of his mail-car; then, he checked to make sure no-one was around to hear his clandestine conversation.

It was an accepted fact, in Ed's world, that White men spit on, beat, insulted, and even killed Colored people as a regular course of action; their choice for murder was usually lynching. The rationale for a mob lynching could be anything - factual or imagined. Real crime or wrong-doing had very little to do with the lynching of a Negro.

Ed knew for a fact that lynching and other terrible mistreatments of Negroes, such as the fire at Uncle DaDa's house, were sins committed by some White people just for entertainment. As a young man, it never occurred to Ed that he actually might be able to do anything to stop that type of killing or activity; it was just a part of life in the South as he knew it to be. What could he do, as one person, to change something that was going on long before he was born? That was a social justice issue, and social justice was not the responsibility of a single individual; Congress passed laws for that purpose. It was not Ed's responsibility! Or was it?

Ed remembered...

It was a conversation with Mr. and Mrs. Keys that caused some of Ed's forgotten memories, from the depths of his childhood, to purge forth to a priority space in the consciousness of his adulthood. Sights he had seen, words he had heard, scents he had smelled suddenly became a concoction stirring in his belly. The imbedded knowledge regurgitated inside Ed's system, and left a sour taste in his mouth. Ed began to feel weak as the reality of the truth he was learning, in real time, focused his memories of a time long past. It was harder and harder for Ed to ignore his feelings since he was becoming aware of certain facts. His perspective was changing…

Ed was an avid reader…

As a child, Ed could often be found sitting under a tree reading a book while his sister and brothers were running around getting into trouble. Mr. and Mrs. Keys began to supply Ed with his primary reading materials, and he absorbed everything he read like a sponge. Ed was riveted by the information he read, there was so much he didn't comprehend. He felt an inner anger he could not articulate – let alone decipher who the anger should be directed toward. His brain became a storehouse of new information, which contributed to a time of enlightenment; Ed began to think deeply about things he never really gave serious thought to before.

Ed became aware…

Ed's increasing awareness began to affect his behavior in little ways - in ways he found hard to explain to anyone. It was information which Ed learned from a book he borrowed from Mr. and Mrs. Keys that made him turn down a suggestion from Suellen to take their children on a picnic. Ed gave Suellen a hasty "NO!" She gave him a puzzled look.

"OK." Suellen stammered, and walked out of the room. Ed saw tears swell in Suellen's eyes; still, he never gave her the reason for his abrupt reply. Ed only knew that he could never go on another picnic, but he couldn't explain his reaction – not even to himself. Ed considered… Maybe it would feel better for him if a picnic were called something else – another name: a barbecue, a cookout, or a pleasure outing – anything but a picnic.

In his reading Ed learned the history behind society's innocent, polite, family fun-filled gathering. He read that the picnic, which he always loved, really began as a *pic-a-nigger* day when: White folks brought their families to a picturesque grassy area for a community gathering, special food was prepared, the local White men (sometimes even the officials of the government and local law enforcement) picked a '*Nigger*' to hang on a nearby tree, and all the White people (women and children alike) watched and enjoyed the spectacle.

Many slaves were gathered up and forced to witness the lynching while the White *picnic* attendees indulged in the decadence of their senses. In this public forum, the initiators of the *picnic* actually seemed to luxuriate in the misery of Black people: the sounds of their guttural moans, the volume of their screams, and the sight of their grieving bodies sprawled prostrate on the ground crying - begging for the life of a loved one. Although lynching was no longer the dictating force behind the social event, Ed could not empty his head of the emotionally shattering images.

The more facts Ed understood about discrimination the harder it was for him to find comfort in the presence of his own race – even some members of his family. Like a magnet Ed's attention was drawn to obvious facts, which he previously saw without seeing, heard without hearing. His new awareness would no longer allow Ed to observe certain occurrences with indifference.

For instance, he couldn't look at the abundance of Mulatto children born to Negro women without the obvious question galloping through his head... Who raped who? How many Mulatto children were born of White women? Ed had to conclude that it seemed obvious that White men raped Negro women; it was not the White women who had the Mulatto babies... Ed's thoughts pounded unremittingly at his consciousness.

If Colored people were so much like filthy animals - dirty, unclean and unkempt, why did the White men rape the Colored man's woman? White men claimed that their pure White - supposedly virtuous, chaste, and desirable women were the Colored man's ultimate desire; in fact, a Colored man could get killed if the White man even thought the Colored man looked at his White woman. Yet, the countryside was sprinkled with fatherless mixed-race Negroes such as Jazmine Sage's little baby. Who was coveting who? Agonizing thoughts kept resurfacing. Ed's headache reoccurred; he reprimanded the remnant of his old self - the persona that was still hidden in the recesses of his brain… The egoism that seeped into his thinking tried to convince Ed that he should believe all the things he was taught in his youth; he could not yet totally restrain all of his early teachings. However, whenever Ed viewed those teaching from his new understanding, he was baffled…

Ed thought specifically of J.K. Sage's daughter, Jazmine… Did the White man who raped that beautiful Colored child think he was sleeping with an animal? Would that same man also have had sex with a horse, a dog, a cow? That notion was just plain nasty! Ed was beginning to feel so confused; all of this segregation stuff presented so many contradictions. Ed rubbed his fingertips across his pain-contorted forehead; he imagined the racial dilemma in the United States as a festering sore, on the tip of Uncle Sam's nose.

Ed questioned his old self…

"What do Southern White folks want the world to think about them and their land?" Ed asked of his old self. Although the character of the old Ed had gradually become more subordinate, the moral fiber of the evolving new Ed still struggled with the last vestiges of his old thoughts. After all, the childhood teachings were long-term residents in his makeup that were hard for the evolving Ed to evict from his mind.

Then, the answer to his inner question popped into Ed's head as if it were a direct reply from his old self. Ed thought… Die-hard Southerners would love for the rest of the world to only see: the early morning dew when it glistened on the healing Goldenrod growing from the fertile ground, the lazy *Old Man River* as it simply rolled along, the attitude of Uncle Remus *(There's a Bluebird on my shoulder- it's the truth - it's natural – everything is satisfactual)* to represent the happy singing Colored folks on the plantation, and their intense compassion for the Confederate Flag.

Ed's evolving inner self was becoming an enlightened spirit; that was the spirit that challenged the presumptions of his former outer self - whose concepts and beliefs were no longer adequate… Ed posed more questions to himself… What was the sinister reality that was underneath the outer cover of Southern beauty, dedication, and splendor?

The consistent mental confrontations with his old self left Ed fatigued because he honestly knew those examples of southern existence were simply facades starved of the real sustenance of southern life - which he was discovering was deeply grounded in racism. Ed wondered if he would live long enough to see the ugly green pimpled skin of racism yanked off to expose, to the world, the frog-like underbelly of the Jim Crow system which covered: the land where he was born, the country he went to war for, the land of The Stars and Stripes, the Land of the Free, the land he so desperately wanted to be proud of.

Ed backtracked through his childhood memories, and withdrew a forgotten recollection from his tenth year. He realized that he personally knew some White people who had killed, or spoke of killing, someone they called 'a Niggra' because of a perceived action that ignited an explosion of anger. Like a bottle of Coke, shaken before opening, some White people seemed to become uncontrollable, uncontainable, and capable of killing any Negro in their path; otherwise those same people seemed to lead normal lives.

Ed speculated…

What made anyone so violent - capable of treating another human with so much hatred? Was there a dark evil side that some of us are born with, or did people learn to be that mean? Ed speculated… Was there a caustic ingredient, a DNA, within a person that caused them to dislike other people with such vengeance? He wondered if he had that kind of behavior hidden deep inside of his being. "I don't think so." Ed answered his own question. But, Ed still had more questions… Was it the same thing if he saw wrongdoing without doing anything about it?

Ed evoked the past…

Ed remembered a time when his Uncle Matthew stopped by his house, and hastily grabbed his father's elbow to pull him onto the back porch to talk in private. Uncle Matthew was talking very fast as if he couldn't catch his breath while he tried to whisper at the same time. Ed was ten years old when he hid under the window sill, inside his bedroom, where he could listen to his father and Uncle Matthew's conversation. He heard the entire exchange without being seen.

"They done killed that Colored man who hired himself out on da Lynch farm helping tu pic da 'bacco. He twas da only Colored workin' wit' da farmers today. You know how old man Lynch have extra farm work dis time a year; he'll take on whoever come first to bring da crop in." Uncle Matthew was panting like a winded runner; he was holding his right side with one hand as if in pain while he supported himself on the porch rail with his left hand. Uncle Matthew's face was flushed with red blotches, and sweat dripped from his hair.

"Da Colored man worked real good all during da morning; fact twas, I heard he was saying dat he hope Mr. Lynch would let'im come back. So anyways - all da field hands took a water break at da same time; dhey was all drinking water outta da dipper dat hang on'a nail by da well. The problem come 'cause dere was only one dipper. You know don't nobody keep more dan one dipper at deir well. Anyways, da Colored man stood back – respectful like - til everyone else finish wit'da dipper 'fore he drank; just like he s'possed to." Ed's father just stood still and listened to his brother.

"Den, one'a da other hir'd hands gotta attitude." Uncle Matthew continued breathlessly. "Hear tell it twas dat red headed boy from the Killgen family. 'Member him? He was in high school da same time we was; he never did finish school far as I know." Uncle Matthew stopped talking long enough to get a confirmation from Ed's father that he understood who he was talking about.

"You know how dat Killgen boy always a bully." Matthew continued. "Well, Killgen 'cided he want'a second drink, and dat twas his right – 'cause he was White - ta drink again, 'fore any Nigga drank any." Uncle Matthew explained... his words in staccato.

"Fr'm what I 'ear, the Colored man had thought er'body was finish. Anyways, he had already started ta get his drink. So, Mr. Hot-Tempered-Killgen knocked da dipper outa his hand. Da dipper accident'ly hit one'a da other workers, who figur'd dat the Colored man hit him on purpose. But, twas just an accident. For real! Well, dis free-fo-all broke out; dey all jumped on da Colored man. Dey say dey beat him!

Dey beat him ta death! He died! Da man died right dere, an they just laughed!" Matthew said.

Matthew slid down into a sitting position on the porch steps; his legs refused to hold his body upright because they were shaking in convulsions. Ed could not see any of this, but he heard the thumping sounds on the porch steps.

"Old man Lynch t'wer't there when it first happen, but it t'was him that called the sheriff to come. Sheriff Jim come, and he laughed with hir'd hands; then, Sheriff Jim help ta throw the body intu the Dan River." Uncle Matthew continued. "Sheriff Jim say the body's bound to wash up sooner or later; he say tha's one less Niggra to worry 'bout."

Ed's father was listening intensely; he just shook his head, and every now and then he made grunts as if he was robbed of exclamation. Then, Ed heard his father utter his first words. He simply asked Matthew, "What'd old man Lynch say?"

"He seem a little upset; he say it's a shame, 'cause the Niggra twas such a hard worker... Old man Lynch say he hate ta loose him 'cause he don't hav't pay the Niggra hand as much as he do the others." Matthew replied.

Ed knew for a fact that no-one was ever arrested for the crime. He remembered hearing about a body washing up, down river, several months later. He remembered the jokes he heard, about the killing, when he went to school. Ed remembered how he pretended to laugh with the boys, sons of the redhead Killgen, and others he called friends. Ed remembered how at ten years old he wondered, to himself, why the incident had turned into a murder.

At the age of personal development, his pre-teenage years, Ed tried to understand this conflict with humanity thru the examination of his own feelings. There were so many things Ed wanted to talk to somebody about... Instead Ed stored most of his childhood questions in his subconscious. But, in his adult years, those suppressed questions started to scratch at the entryway to Ed's mind, like an impatient dog that needed to be let out of its confinement to relieve itself or burst.

Why did so many White people have such an uncontrollable anger about Colored people in general? Why did some White people think they possessed a superior birth-right when they had absolutely nothing to do with the placement of their own birth? Ed chuckled to himself as he considered the absurdity of the idea... What did they think babies did, have a little pre-birth talk with God? Ed's imagination played out such a pre-birth dialogue.

> *God, I want you to send me down to earth as a pure White child, born to pure White parents because I know that White people are your master race. I will help you keep the race pure by killing those on earth who are not White according to your plan... OK Lord?*

Ed shook his head at the concept.

"What else could the people, who believe in racial cleansing, be thinking?" Ed uttered as he talked aloud to himself. It was like a wrestling match, in his mind, as he tried to understand people who seemed to have a need to ridicule and abuse others. He concluded that it was not just about Negroes and White people. That sort of callousness was not just a racial thing. It occurred to Ed that the same cruelty could be observed in: husbands who beat their wives, bullies in the schoolyard, menacing co-workers, fighting siblings, even people who tortured animals...

Ed felt compelled...

Ed continued to meditate on the subject - he couldn't seem to let it go; he couldn't get it out of the crevices of his brain. Sometimes Ed felt as if there were chiggers under his skin, causing an unbearable itch - and him with no way to scratch. Ed watched and listened to the Colored people that he came in contact with on Price Road; in addition, he watched and listened closely to the members of the White citizenry. Ed was compelled to continue to look for answers - the reason for his own uneasiness...

Ed began to understand...

Ed understood that he could not see the total picture as much as he tried. He was not privy to what was hidden underneath the smiling faces he saw on the Negroes he observed; he could not see the deep agony, the sorrow and sadness, the fear and loneliness. There was one thing Negroes knew about themselves, and Ed came to understand - that they were very good actors; techniques passed down through generations had proven to be a source of survival - the Shakespearian mask of tragedy.

The outward appearance of indifference had, with practice, become almost second nature to most Negroes. Dancing, music, singing, and even shouting relieved much of their pain. A perceived scenario of happiness seemed to be apparent to those outside of the racial experience. However, for those who shared the experience, which preceded understanding, the soulful music provided a gut retching ritual - a means of sharing their mutually suppressed emotions through the melodies, rhythms, tones and harmonies. The music became compositions of indirect conversation.

It didn't matter if they were making the music personally, dancing, listening, or making love to it; whether it was jazz, spiritual, or the blues, music provided a life saving floodgate for the emotionally contained, hard pressed, and hard working Colored people. There was a choice of musical outlets on Price Road, between the churches and the nightclubs; it just depended on the mood, personal taste, or upbringing that determined which environment the people chose to release their pent-up feelings. Since the need to release those feelings regularly was a must, the 'gut-bucket' blues and swinging jazz on Saturday nights and the spirit of the gospel beat on Sunday mornings flowed seamlessly along Price Road; the lyrics were the only apparent distinction. Ed understood that he had no way of knowing the extent of the undercurrent of emotion that existed in the Colored community, even with his close observation.

And, Ed understood that he could not explain or blame himself for everything his forefathers did. He began to understand that he was responsible for his own actions...

The church ladies said... *"The eyes of the Lord are in every place, beholding the evil and the good."* Proverbs 15: 3

The old folks said... *One can choose to be in a good mood, or one can choose to be in a bad mood.*

METAMORPHOSIS

Uncle DaDa's house fire was a life altering event for Ed; it brought to the surface the change that was already in the process of developing in his character. Ed and his wife, Suellen, attended church as usual, with their children, on Sunday – the day after the fire. Ed smiled at the members of the congregation as they greeted his family. Church was crowded; nevertheless, Ed had a profound feeling of being isolated. He was surrounded by relatives, ex-classmates, co-workers, neighbors. It was a congregation of people that he grew up with, in a church that he had attended all his life; nevertheless, Ed felt an almost uncontrollable need: to stand in the front of the church, to decry their dishonesty to God right there in church, to scream out loud! Instead, he sat with his head bowed in silence; his heart pounded so hard he could feel the beating in his own ears. Ed timidly questioned God, in a private conversation.

"God, how do ya feel about y'ur children treating y'ur other children like they do? We all are your children aren't we Lord? Do ya love some of us more than others? Don't each life have value?" Ed begged for God to talk back to him.

As a father, Ed reflected about his compassion for his own children. He loved them, but not one more than the other. Sometimes, like all children, Ed's children fought with each other and did all sorts of silly things to get attention; however, Ed would never let one mistreat or kill the other. Surely God, the Heavenly Father that God was, could handle such sibling conflicts better than he - a lowly mortal.

"I pray God, help me ta understand" Ed muttered under his breath. His wife heard him, and softly put her hand on his arm as she too bowed her head. Suellen's woman's intuition told her that her husband was troubled, but she could not figure out precisely what his concerns were about. Suellen surmised that Ed's preoccupation had something to do with the fire at Uncle DaDa's, but she knew that was only part of the story. She had noticed some disconnect for several years. As a concerned wife, Suellen was aware that there were times when Ed needed to be alone with his thoughts. Those were the times she let him be... Although Suellen wished Ed would share whatever it was that had his mind in a clutch, she was a patient woman who loved her husband. She knew Ed was a sensitive and intuitive man, which was one of the attributes that endeared him to her; therefore, Suellen waited for Ed to tell her what was festering in his soul. She wanted to talk about *IT*, no matter what *IT* was... Meanwhile, with his eyes tightly closed, Ed continued to talk to hold a private conversation with God.

"I know you're busy God, and I don't mean ta keep you from the important work you have ta do; still, I'd really appreciate it if you give me some wisdom, knowledge, 'n insight. There are some things going on down here on your earth that I just don't understand, 'n I'm trying... I'm really trying hard!" Ed sent his request to God telepathically.

After the church service on that Sunday, the men of the congregation stood together outside on the church lawn - as was their routine. The women greeted each other for 'women talk' while they discreetly pulled on their latex foundation girdles or adjusted their garter belts. The teenagers divided into their boy-girl social groups, and the younger children ran around the churchyard playing 'catch-me-if-you-can'. The women watched the little ones apprehensively, hoping the little girls wouldn't dirty their Sunday best clothes.

No-one was ever in a hurry to leave church after the service was over. That was the time for their weekly sociable small group gathering. The pastor and his wife floated from one group to another - as a good host would. Ed walked over to the group of men already standing together on the front lawn of the church. The men, of assorted ages, were laughing heartily; they were slapping their legs with extreme glee and gaiety. As Ed joined them, the group of male parishioners shook his hand, friendly-slapped him on his back, and anxiously included Ed in on the reason for their joviality.

"We did it! Yessa! We burnt da damm house down! Ya shoud'a seen dem Niggras run. Bet d'ay know da n'xt time not tu mess wid one'a our women!"

It was immediately clear to Ed exactly what they were talking about; he suddenly felt lightheaded and sick to his stomach. After what he considered an ample time, Ed politely excused himself from the conversation; he gathered his family and tried to dispel his sense of desolation as he drove home.

Ed cried out in silence to God. Lord these are people who say they are your children! They are in church every Sunday. They profess their salvation - their born again experience, and they believe their good works are being stored in Heaven because they say they work in service to you. Ed lamented... His soul ached. Still, Ed thought, those same people set fires and lynch people. God, are you satisfied with the church attendance, tithes, and the confessions they put forth in your name? Is that all it takes to be a good Christian – to be saved? Did God hear him? Ed wanted an immediate answer.

Ed could not stop his mental jogging back through time, to his high school history classes. He reflected on what he knew about Thomas Jefferson who was: a contributor to the writing of the Constitution (the political framework for the country), the Secretary of State for George Washington, the Vice President of the United States under President Adams, the third United States President, and the Governor of Virginia; nevertheless, to his shame Jefferson was also a slave owner who took sexual advantage of his female slaves. Jefferson did not have a formal affiliation with a religion. Did that mean that he had an inner conflict with the inconsistency of his own actions and resisted facing God head on? Constitutionally he supported freedom for all; however, Jefferson never gave his own children, who were born into slavery, their freedom. Did Jefferson believe his own children were beast of burden? Nobody knew what Jefferson was thinking... Certainly Ed couldn't imagine the Jeffersonian thinking process.

"I can't hear you; your actions are too loud." Ed's father always said. Those words, spoken years ago, still gave Ed plenty to think about as he became more vigilant in his growing obsession of people watching.

Ed always enjoyed his history classes when he was in school. Books about the lives of people, places, and events in history were always interesting to him. Ed pictured the events as if a movie were playing against the background of time whenever he read the textbooks his classmates found boring. If it were possible to travel back in years to talk to the residents of that time, Ed determined that he would like to talk to Thomas Jefferson. He had so many questions to ask him; mean-while, since meeting with Jefferson was an impossibility, Ed just prayed a simple, silent prayer.

"Please Lord help me to understand my fellow man. Most of all help me to understand me, so that I might know how to do your will. I want to live my life the way you want me to. For this I pray in Jesus' name." Ed asked all this of God thru tightly closed eyes and lips.

The old folks said... *Actions speak louder than words.*

Ed learned a lot that Sunday, too much in fact. Between the laughter and the reciting of the events surrounding the fire Ed was able to discern, from the man-talk, the incident that precipitated the vigilante action. One of the young men had been dating Lola, a woman who had a reputation for running around with many men. Most people in town, who knew Lola, considered the young woman as a scalawag. In Lola's devious way she thought she was able to keep her flirtations hidden from her primary boyfriend, whoever he was at the time; usually the boyfriend actually made the choice to overlook the truth that he knew about her. One afternoon Lola misjudged her time; her current main man couldn't find her. When her boyfriend did track her down, he found her coming out of a storehouse in a neighbor's backyard.

"Lola, wh't in da world is you doing in dere?" he asked. He really didn't want to know the truthful answer, and Lola was not about to give it to him. Shaking like a leaf on a tree in the mist of a tornado, the tarnished but voluptuous girl invented a plausible story - right on the spot.

Lola stammered something about being scared which she ascribed to '*some big Niggra man.*' The more questions her boyfriend asked, the more Lola cried. Between an emotional display of tears, Lola told her boyfriend that she had hidden in the storehouse out of fear. Actually, she had been with her lover who was still hiding behind the boxes in the storehouse.

"Wha'd he look like? I'll take care o'him; he'll neve' scare ya a'gan." the angry boyfriend asked.

Lola continued to feign tears while she covered her face with both hands. Her boyfriend kept prodding until finally Lola spurted out something from between her fingers...

"He twas tall, but not too tall! He twas dark, but not real dark! He 'ad black hair! He 'ad muscles! Look strong in da arms... Oh Yeah! He 'ad a deep voice... Real scary!

"Wha'd he say t'ya? Wha'd he do t'ya?" he asked.

"Ah can't 'member!" Lola cried louder, still covering her face. "Ah'se to scared to 'member!" she whimpered.

The boyfriend wanted to believe her although his instincts warned him that she was lying. As a man, an offended boyfriend, he had to *appear* to protect his woman's honor. It didn't take long for the enraged young man to recruit three of his drinking buddies. They all knew the girl was lying, but they didn't need much of an excuse to punish a 'Niggra'; it would be fun. The four vigilantes stopped to drink some moonshine before they were on their way.

While the small mob rode on horseback, through the back-woods to Price Road, they tried to figure out their mode of operation as they passed the Mason jar back and forth. In a drunken stupor, they each contributed sloppy thoughts to their collective thinking:

"Din't she say it t'was a *big* Niggra?"

"Dem Ashford boys is big – must'a been one'f 'dem."

"Got some nerve scar'ng ma woman! We 'otta burn da house down!"

"Right! That 'otta teach da Niggra's a lesson! Don't look at our women 'else we'll burn ya house down. Down! Down! Ya hear me? We'll burn it down!"

It didn't matter that no-one from the Ashford household had been to town for weeks; nothing mattered except the fabricated need for revenge, the appearance of preserving a white woman's honor. Actually, any Niggra would do.

It was an apocalyptic air as the tall pine trees bordering the back-woods seemed to part allowing the four galloping horses onto Uncle DaDa Ashford's backyard. Fortunately Uncle DaDa spotted the group as they emerged from the woods in the back of his house. DaDa knew immediately that there was going to be trouble; it was a learned instinct since he didn't even hear the mantra the horsemen sang.

"Gonna teach the Niggra's a lesson... Gonna teach the Niggra's a lesson."

Ed understood, without a doubt, what Deacon Riley meant when he and Suellen stood together watching Uncle DaDa's house burn. Ed's church members were the SNAKES! Ed could hardly contain himself when he heard the story as it was told at church by the church members who participated.

Not one of the four drunken mobsters saw the family escape out the front door. They didn't know whether or not any of the Ashford family had been killed in the fire… didn't care who knew they had set the fire. They stuck their chests out with pride as they pranced around the church lawn relating the story; it was like a notch on their belts, and everybody knew that the law was on their side. One of the boys was Sheriff Jim's son, another was the minister's grandson; they all knew they would never be arrested.

That night Ed couldn't hold his emotions inside himself any longer; he opened his heavy heart to his wife.

"Suellen, did you hear that those boys at church were the ones who set Uncle DaDa's house on Price Road on fire? They were talking about it after church today, and everybody was laughing - they thought it was funny." he said haltingly. Ed had to stand up, he began to pace the room; his legs wouldn't let him sit still.

"How awful!" Suellen replied. She turned to look at Ed, directly scrutinizing her husband's face. Suellen could see Ed's frustration: the deep furrow in his brow, the squint of his eyes, the steeple his pointer fingers connected to form under his nose as his hands interlocked to cover his mouth, and the suppressed groan that was stuck somewhere in his throat.

"Those poor people with no place to live now…. Why? Fo what?" Suellen said when Ed told her the story as he heard it…

"Lawd, everybody in town know that scarlet woman ain't got no honor to be salvaged." Suellen said in genuine horror, "Everybody knows she's a habitual liar!"

Ed looked intently at his wife; her reaction gave him confidence, maybe he could share his thinking with her. Without muttering a word out loud, Ed reached for Suellen's hand; he relaxed his shoulders, inhaled deeply and sent God another silent prayer…

Lord, I sho would be grateful if I could talk to Suellen without feeling like my thinking is wrong. I'm really trying to understand what I should do... It would be such a comfort to have someone to share my thoughts with in a purposeful way. I'd like to be able to say to Suellen – *Let's talk about <u>IT</u>...* In Jesus's name I pray...

Ed looked into Suellen's eyes; behind their blueness he saw, for the first time, compassion as deep as the ocean. It had to have been there all the time; maybe he was so submersed in his own thoughts that he never noticed. He began to tell his wife some of the rumblings going through his mind. Suddenly Ed couldn't stop talking; it was as if he were a dam that burst...

Suellen listened; then, she tried to convey her thoughts to Ed. The beliefs they both had overlapped each other with tender expression; their conversation was revealing. The couple discovered so much about each other; Ed's lonely sense of desolation began to disappear as he held Suellen's hands and they prayed together in agreement.

Ed once heard the old folks say, *"You are either a leader, or a follower. If you're not either one... then get out of the way."* It was a single thought that refused to retreat from his brain. Ed thought... How does that apply to me? Maybe I need to sleep on it. He felt exhausted and decided - clarity of thought will come with the morning.

The following day, Monday, Ed went to work as usual, but he was not the same person; he approached the job he loved with a new prospective. Ed concluded that he wasn't a follower; therefore, he had to figure out how to lead, 'cause he couldn't get out of the way.

"Nobody is going to listen to me about anything; I'm just 'Ed the mailman'. Nobody listens to me except my children." Ed said to himself with amusement. "Ok, that's it! I'll lead my own family!"

Ed began to think about how he could be a real leader in his own household. He reflected – the Bible said that the man was the head of his house... Ed considered how important a role that was. Ed focused on the qualities of a real man; he concluded: a real man commands respect - based on love not fear, a good father sets the moral example – by his own actions, and the foundation of family values should be established by the father of the family according to God's Covenant.

Suddenly Ed felt more confident about what he should do… He decided to discuss his ideas with Suellen. It felt good to know that he had a life partner with whom he could talk to openly. Finally, he could talk about <u>*IT*</u>! Ed felt the weight of his concerns lift from his shoulders. This must be how a butterfly felt when it emerged from a cocoon… As Ed drove down Price Road that Monday, he felt enlightened – no longer confused. Ed recognized racism as an illness, a disease with causes; he discovered he did not have to be sick.

The church ladies said… *You show your love for God through your actions toward other people.*

TELEVISION

On Monday morning, the day after Ed discovered who the culprits were who burned down Uncle DaDa's house, he spotted Deacon Riley walking down Price Road toward Spring Church. He stopped his car to talk with the Deacon who sadly informed him that Uncle DaDa's entire family had left Price Road on Sunday. The Ashford's grown children, who lived in Canada, had come immediately after the fire and moved their parents away. Deacon Riley discretely wiped a tear off his cheek as he handed an envelope to Ed which contained a forwarding address, in Canada, for Uncle DaDa. As Ed looked at Uncle DaDa's new address, he felt his heart plummet; it seemed as if an arrow had penetrated Ed's bubble and dispelled his optimism. Uncle DaDa was one of Ed's favorite people on Price Road... Ed excused himself from any further conversation with Deacon Riley; he felt the blood flow suddenly away from his head. Ed wondered if his ashen face revealed feelings he could not yet articulate to Deacon Riley; therefore, Ed simply said, "Thank you Deacon."

Although he was saddened about the news he heard from Deacon Riley, Ed was in a rush to get home at the end of the day. He could hardly contain himself; he had so much to tell his wife. Some things seemed much clearer to him, and he could hardly wait to share his thinking with Suellen.

It was a fact that Jim Crow laws were legal in the South. Even Ed's favorite President, Franklin D. Roosevelt, showed his acceptance of the Jim Crow laws when he proclaimed himself a transplanted Georgian - without condemning that state's treatment of colored citizens, and Georgia's significant reputation for the vast number of lynchings of colored people. But, just because the United States laws allowed the mistreatment of some of its citizens didn't make it morally right. Ed realized that even the most respected lawmakers were easily swayed by political and economical reasoning; morality sometimes did not even make the list of the top ten in the governing process.

As a student, and later as a parent, Ed did not know the behind-the-scene manipulations of the Leaksville Board of Education; he did not even have a rudimentary understanding of the ramifications of legalized separation throughout the South. Ed never questioned the system; that was all he ever knew. He had not understood that when the administrators spoke of co-equal, or separate, the legalized active school policy actually screamed otherwise.

Ed discovered, through a televised news interview with Negro students in the South, how text books were really distributed. The students interviewed shattered Ed's illusion about public education when they shared the experiences they had while attending a segregated school. They told how their textbooks were first used by students at the White schools; then, the books were passed down to the Colored schools after they were: used up, torn up, and outdated. Nevertheless, the school officials actually called this process '**equal**'. Ed came to the inescapable appreciation of the true importance and value of Mr. and Mrs. Keys' home library, and the importance of the television.

Because of the news reports they saw on television, and the books Ed began to share with his wife, Ed and Suellen began having extensive conversations. They discussed many major issues such as: the Brown verses The Board of Education decision about school segregation, the Emmett Till murder in Mississippi, and the bus boycott in Alabama. Because of their evolving level of communication, Ed and Suellen began to comprehend the truth of segregation.

"Do you realize that everyone has a television set now? We are able to *see* things on television that we only heard about before. I think a television-in-every-home has the power to change public opinion." Ed said to Suellen while they watched the 6 o'clock news.

"Ya're right. People act different when they know they're being watched; they can't hide what they're doing in the backwoods 'cause the TV camera catches them in their lies." Suellen agreed.

Ed knew his prediction about the impact of the television was true; he could see that it was already happening. In September of 1957 the citizens of the world saw televised reports of: the Governor of Arkansas on television as he stood in the front door of a Little Rock School to keep Colored children out; Althea Gibson, the first Negro tennis player to win a Wimbledon singles title; retired baseball player, Jackie Robinson, interviewed as a Vice President of Chock-Full-O-Nuts; Eisenhower inaugurated as the United States President; Charles Steele, Fred Shuttlesworth, and Martin Luther King when they established the [SCLC] Southern Christian Leadership Conference. The television reports revealed the racial rumblings, primarily in America's South, that were like a gaseous stomach on the verge of severe diarrhea... As uncomfortable as it was, as ugly as it was to look at, diarrhea was sometimes necessary to clean out a system in order to prevent an ultimate death... It was a fact that both Ed and Suellen agreed upon while they watched America' vile excretion on the evening news.

Ed heard racial rhetoric all his life from the people he respected; he trusted those people: mother, father, relatives, preacher, and teachers. Was it possible that his was taught what his teachers honestly believed because that was what they themselves were taught?

Ed and Suellen were sure that there were other White people who, like themselves, were unaware of their own mis-education. Ed knew that the mis-taught beliefs were the source of a generational illness so grounded and imbedded in some of the older White folks that they became extremely defensive whenever anyone challenged them about those beliefs... They were people who could not even identify when they began to have such prejudiced ideas any more than they could remember when they learned to breathe. Ed forgave all those people as soon as the thought entered his mind; it was not fair to judge someone because they didn't know what they didn't know. Ed thought the lack of awareness in the world would change because of the televised reports; the facts were coming forth for all to see.

"I guess our parents did the best they could based on what they knew, and they only knew what they were taught." Suellen told Ed.

"Yeah... It's for sure television is going to change the intellectual horizon; everyone will be able to see the information for their selves." Ed predicted.

Ed and Suellen began to realize the importance of their job as parents... Parents had a great responsibility; they had to expose their children to a variety of information and experiences to develop healthy viewpoints, just as they exposed children to a variety of nutritional foods to develop healthy bodies.

"Maybe if we taught our own children that all of us on this earth are kindred spirits it might have a ripple effect like a pebble thrown into the water." Suellen suggested - Ed agreed.

Ed realized that all people had the same needs and desires, regardless of what color they were. Everybody wanted basically the same thing in their lives. Negro children played the same games as his White children. Ed knew this because he personally got to know so many Negroes through his job on Price Road, and he discovered how much they had in common. Ed accepted the fact that there were good and bad people in his race, and there were good and bad people in the Negro race too. Ed realized if it were not for his job he would have had no real contact with any Negroes.

"If people of different races got to know each other personally, and learned to respect each other as equal human beings in the sight of God, they could work together to make this world a better place for all to live… The key was **'to get to know'** each other, and not to prejudge other people based on assumptions." Ed said to Suellen.

It was indeed an epiphany moment for Ed; he felt a positive surge in his soul, and he knew that he was onto something important.

"Honey, do our children know any Negroes?" Ed asked Suellen.

"Well, I have seen some on the street, but I don't think they have ever even spoken to any Negroes…" Suellen replied thoughtfully.

"They've seen the girls… I'm sorry; I should say the ladies that clean at their school. But, I don't think they come in to work 'til school is closed… No, guess not… What yo thinking?" she asked Ed.

"I was thinking that it's hard for people to have an understanding and a respect for other people, who are different from them, if they don't know each other; 'specially when they were raised to believe, through the teachings of parents and society, that they're the #1 people in the world – the master race - superior to all other races." Ed said. His thoughts seeped pass his lips slowly.

"My parents, I guess yours too, taught us that Colored people were like animals - even had tails under their pants. We were taught that Colored people were nonentities. They were to be made fun of…

'member all the racial jokes we heard all our lives." Ed said as panorama of some of the things he recently learned flashed through his head.

Ed remembered seeing Black Jockey lawn statues; a lot of White people had them; in fact, there were still some around. The statues were used as a status symbol of the privileged master class - implying that they, the pure White people, should be served at all times - even though they no longer possessed slaves. Although the White community used the display of the lawn statues as a massive statement of disrespect to colored people, it was something that Ed never paid any attention to. When he noticed Mrs. Keys kept one of those statues on her porch, not on the lawn, it dawned on Ed that he had never seen one of those statues at a Colored person's home. He commented about that fact to Mrs. Keys; then, she told Ed the true history of the figure...

"A statue like this was commissioned to be made at the request of George Washington; it was his way to pay tribute to a young Negro boy, by the name of Jocko Graves, for his bravery in holding a lantern and the horses for the troops while they crossed the Delaware River." Mrs. Keys told Ed.

"When the soldiers returned to the shoreline, the boy stood in place - frozen to death while his hands still griped the reins of the horses in the ice and snow. Because of the young boy's bravery and commitment, Washington's troops were inspired to fight harder." Mrs. Keys continued.

"The death of the Jocko Graves saddened George Washington. He said that Jocko had made the supreme sacrifice - he gave his life. Washington's commission of the statute was definitely not a derogatory statement; it was his way of paying tribute to the brave young Jocko. In subsequent years White people managed to turn the statute into something derogatory." Mrs. Keys said just before Mr. Keys came onto the porch. Mr. Keys heard the last part of their conversation, and he was eager to add to Ed's knowledge and understanding.

"Another thing," Mr. Keys said, as he interrupted the conversation, "those statues were used to signal to the run-away slaves as to where the safe houses of the Underground Railroad were. A 'Black Jocko' on the lawn, with a green scarf on the outstretched arm, meant that it was safe for the run-a-way slave to stop. A red scarf signaled that there was danger, keep going - do not stop." Mr. Keys was talking as if he was riding the horse of explanation on a long journey. He started out with his words in a slow and measured trot.

"Can you imagine how the sight of a green scarf made the hearts of the escapee jump for joy and how scared they must have felt when they saw a red scarf?" Mr. Keys had a good start. His speech pattern increased in speed. He loosened any restraints he might have heretofore felt; he began to speak as fast as he could. Mr. Keys crouched; his eyes scanned the area around him, in a watchful searching mode, as his body seemed to transport into the time and place he spoke of. Mr. Keys spoke with force; he was on a full gallop through the history of slavery.

Ed learned a lot from the Keys that day. As his eyes of perspective began to open, Ed remembered the many things he and other White children were told when they were too young to know any better.

"We can't use da same wat'r fountain ax the Coloreds 'cause they so nasty. Might make us sick'n we'd die." White people said.

Ed shook his head in amazement at the thought that went through his head at that moment. "Explain this to me… Why do White people allow Negroes to cook, clean, and wash for them? A whole lot of White children have actually been raised by Colored nannies who did everything for the children - including breast feeding… It just don't make sense." Ed said to Suellen.

"The people who told us that Colored people were filthy are the same people who would allow a dog to kiss them in the face after the dog had just finished licking its own butt, and even let the dog sleep in the bed with them." Ed said. He could not keep himself from shuttering involuntarily when he focused on the realism of that thought.

"They say Colored folk ain't trustworthy; still, they trust them with their food 'n their children's lives… I'd be scared to do that with an untrustworthy, nasty animal… See what I mean Suellen? Do you realize how much we have been mis-taught?" he said.

"Well, there must be something we can do to make things better. We can't know the truth and do nothing; that has to be something like a sin." Suellen said gently as she rubbed Ed's shoulders. "Let's talk about *IT.*"

Ed and Suellen fell asleep, cuddled in each others arms, while still having the same conversation.

The old folks said... *The only thing that is truly yours, that no one can control or take from you, is your attitude.*

The church ladies said... *Sometimes the angels fly so close you can hear their wings flutter; sometimes God just uses regular people.*

FIRST STEPS

"Would you mind if I brought my family over to meet you? My children could play with yours sometime, and I think you 'n my wife would enjoy each other's company." Ed said to Freesia Holly the following Tuesday. Freesia's children were near the same age as his, and Ed and Suellen thought it would be a good first step toward living life with their new point of view. Maybe, in their own small way, they could begin to make a difference in the world.

Freesia was puzzled by the self-invite from Ed, but she couldn't think of a real reason to say no.

"Sure." Freesia replied. The inflection in her voice implied more of a question than an endorsement. Ed ignored the look on her face. Freesia had every reason to be surprised.

The following weekend Ed and his family made a special trip to Price Road to visit Freesia. "This is Suellen, my wife." Ed said. The children ran off together, not needing the formality of an introduction. While the women walked and talked about the flowers and the garden, Ed sat openly on Freesia's porch – reared back - comfortable like. His legs were crossed, right ankle over left knee. His hands were interlocked to hold the back of his head as he rocked back and forth on the green and white cushioned glider; then, Ed realized something... He didn't even care who rode down the road and saw him sitting there... Maybe for the first time in his life, Ed felt *free*. Free. FREE! REALLY FREE!!! It was a feeling of liberation!

Of course Ed knew he was supposed to have been born free, especially because he was born White; still in that space and time he recognized a feeling of euphoria, a spiritual equilibrium, which had to be associated with the feeling of true freedom. Ed thought... *Both the jailer and the jailee are in prison.* Did he hear that someplace, or was that his own wisdom? Ed uncrossed his legs and readjusted himself into the comfort of the cushioned glider on Freesia's front porch. He smiled...

"The children don't want to leave, but we have to go now." Ed said after some respectable time had passed. "We don't want to wear out our welcome."

"Will you come back soon?" Freesia said as she handed Suellen an assortment of cuts from her plants wrapped in a newspaper.

"Sure we will, and I'll bring you my recipe for that green bean casserole." Suellen said as she timidly gave Freesia a friendly good-bye hug and settled into the passenger seat of the car.

The children talked all the way home about how much fun they had; especially when they played on the tire swing hanging from the tree in the back yard. Ed tried to be casual about his question when he asked the children,

"Did you guys notice anything about that family that was different?"

"No... Like what?" his children answered.

"I just wondered if ya noticed that they looked a little different from da other people you know." Ed replied cautiously.

"Yeah Dad, you know you right. They are different, 'member when we waz resting on da ground, looking up at the sky? Well, we waz talking 'bout how their skin is the same color az God's earth, 'n our skin looked more like the clouds floating in the sky. So, we waz pretending that's what we were, we figu'rd that's why we called White. So, we waz pretending to be the clouds. So they waz pretending to be the earth. And, you know how the ground comes in a lot of different shades of brown, well we figu'rd dat's why they called Colored."

Ed's younger son couldn't be quiet any longer; he was fidgeting in his seat from excitement. He wanted to tell his parents the part he liked best about the make-believe play with his new friends.

"Dad, you know how da ground holds things, like da roots hold plants 'n trees 'n things so az they'll grow in place. And you know what Dad? If it wasn't for the earth there prob'ly wouldn't be no clouds... 'Cause you know how da earth holds the water that comes from the clouds, like when it rains, 'til it can 'vaporate and goes back to the clouds." In their obvious excitement, about their pretend play, the children began to talk so fast that Ed could hardly keep up with who was talking. Suellen wore a look of satisfaction as she looked in the back seat and smiled at her children.

"We all learned in school that clouds water the earth, like Mom waters the flowers, to help em grow and stay healthy. It's like dey work together... The whole world is able to exist because of the brown earth 'n white clouds working together... Cool huh!"

"Yeah, that's real cool," Ed replied. "In fact it's *copasetic.*" he added as he drove past Meadow Woods and thought of Tyree Udell, who taught him that word.

"So, when can we go back so we play earth 'n clouds again? That was fun!" the children begged. "Please Daddy Please!"

Ed looked at his wife and they shared a warm smile. They both felt that they were accomplishing something - something small; however, maybe that's what it takes to get a big job done. How do you walk around the world? One step at a time... When he decided to talk about *IT* to Suellen, he took the first step. Ed felt like a leader; they were taking their first steps. It felt good... It felt right...

"Jesus, this is the kind of thing you would do isn't it?" Ed said to himself as he looked toward the sky. In that moment he really felt he had made a personal connection with Jesus.

My God... What could this world be if every man would set this kind of example for his own family? If every man became a leader for civility in his own house, then maybe the next generation would not be so full of hate toward each other.

Ed thought about Mr. Vera, one of the old men who sat on the porch at the store, who was a part of the Black community where his Chinese ancestry was accepted without question while the White community rejected the Chinese and the Japanese people. In fact, the Klu Klux Klan preached hatred for all ethnicities - except their own.

Ed actually knew people, family and neighbors, who were not violent as the KKK but still shared – if not completely at least in part - the same concepts the KKK expounded. Some clandestine members of the KKK appeared to be quiet law abiding citizens; in fact, some even said things like, "I have Negro friends," or "I contribute to the NAACP." It was not uncommon for some White people to exhibit such mock-sincerity because they were trying to impress some prominent or distinguished Negro whom they wanted to impress with their *liberal* acceptance in public - while they hid their true feelings in private.

"I prayed for wisdom, knowledge, and insight... Thank you God..." Ed whispered so softly that only he and God could hear. He was beginning to understand.

"You did hear my prayer didn't you God!" Ed closed his eyes and held his hands in a prayer mode. "Would you look at it as a sin if I let myself feel real smart right now Lord? I'm just so excited!" Ed exclaimed as he whispered into his folded hands. Ed felt on the verge of gloating to himself; he struggled to stop himself from committing what he knew was one of the seven most deadly sins – PRIDE. In spite of himself Ed felt his chest swell with so much pride.

After the children were in bed, Ed pulled his wife onto his lap. "I think my love for you just got deeper - as if it was possible to love you more!" Suellen told Ed. As they sat in that position, they shared their most intimate thoughts, feelings, and dreams - until Ed's leg cramped from the weight of his wife on his leg. They laughed when he almost dumped her on the floor; it had been a long time since there was that much visible frivolity in the house. The children, not yet asleep, felt happy and secure as they snuggled under their covers.

The church ladies said... *Follow the little children.*

The old folks said... *The most important 'ability' is responsibility.*

NOW IS THE TIME

After that first visit to Fressia's home, both Ed and Suellen became regular fixtures on Price Road. Ed truly became more than just a mailman; he and his family had found lifelong friends on Price Road... Friends who shared: joy and sadness, laughter and tears, and events and experiences... There were some bumps along the road, but that was to be expected.

For example: there was the first time that Ed and Suellen invited some of the people, their friends, from Price Road to a *cookout* at their home as guest – not as the cook or the maid. Everyone had such a good time. The children ran around the large yard together and played games of hide and seek, red light, and tag. They threw flat stones into squares drawn in the dirt to play hop scotch. There was the aroma of chicken, hamburger, and steak on the grill while small and large groups of friends were in conversation as others played horseshoes.

Suellen and Ed were definitely conscious of the fact that they were doing something different; the cookout with their Black friends was out of the norm for their neighborhood. They didn't know what to expect as a result of this bold move, but when they decided to host the affair they both were ready to accept whatever the consequences might be.

"Well, I for one am not going to worry about it." Suellen told Ed as she stood at the sink peeling the potatoes for the salad the night before the cookout. "Whatever will be – will be." she said. "I'm not going to pee before my water comes!

Ed laughed... "You're right!" he agreed.

Still, Suellen and Ed couldn't help but notice the reaction of their White neighbors that Sunday: the curtains that seemed to move awkwardly in the front windows of the house across the street, the startled look on the face of the old lady next door as she peeked inquisitively out of her front door, the several cars that drove down the street with the tires rotating in slow motion (only to turn around at the end of

163

the block and drive by again). The shocked reaction of their neighbors gave Ed and Suellen a certain amount of satisfaction… They knew it was not wrong to entertain the people they considered friends in their home; maybe their neighbors would take a hint from them… Wishful thinking…

Nevertheless, there were the threatening anonymous letters and phone calls for the next few weeks, a white doll covered in sticky black tar was left on their back porch, a dead skunk was placed on their front steps, dynamite exploded their mailbox, and the flood of vicious telephone calls was merciless. Suellen and Ed became concerned for their children's safety. Their children were taunted, spit on, and called 'Nigger lovers' at school; in addition, a brick came through the picture window one night. Had they underestimated the cruelty of their friends and neighbors?

"Do you want your child to marry a Niggra'?" Ed and Suellen were asked when their minister and the church council called them in for a special counseling session. Outwardly Ed and Suellen appeared to ignore the perpetrators whereas in reality it was a scary time for everybody in the family. They never told anyone the fact that for over two months after the breakthrough cookout the entire O'Reilly family slept together in the children's bedroom. Ed and Suellen tried not to let their children know the fear they felt, even when they took turns sitting up all night; one on guard with a rifle in the lap while the other slept.

"Ed, you look tired, are you feeling OK?" Professor Wright asked one day.

"Sure, I'm alright." Ed answered, "I just haven't been getting much sleep lately."

"Why not? Is something wrong?"

"Nothing we can't handle."

"Tell me about it."

"Well, it might help to talk to someone about what's happening, but only if you promise not to tell anyone." Professor Bill O. Wright nodded his head ever so slightly, and Ed unburdened his soul… He told the Professor about: the dead skunk, the tar baby doll, and the brick that came through the front window, the telephone calls, the mailbox explosion, and their nightly fear. Fear… FEAR.

Professor Bill O. Wright stood up into his full stature; his eyes narrowed, and he shook Ed's hand.

"I'm glad you told me what was happening to your family." Ed never noticed that the Professor spoke in the past tense… "*Was happening.*" the Professor had said.

The Professor made a few phone calls: Mr. and Mrs. Keys, Pastor Johns, Mr. Laws – the Regional Director of the N.A.A.C.P. In turn they called: NBC, ABC, and CBS, the church ladies, and the old folks on Price Road.

In turn they called: the Governor of North Carolina, the U.S. Attorney General, the local Television News Directors, and the editors of all the local and major newspapers and magazines, the country and city cousins… In turn they called, and called, and called…

The old folks said… *Times change… Change is not to be feared… Time is not to be wasted.*

* * *

"Ed come look! Come see what's on the six o'clock news!" Suellen yelled.

"We are talking with the Governor of North Carolina and Leaksville's Mayor… Sirs, what are you doing to solve the racial discontent problem in your state – in your city?" the news anchor stated into the camera.

"*It's my opinion that some folks want to move this integration thing too fast. It's a coming, but in due time… We have to take it slow… The Colored's in our town are satisfied with our progress. If the outsiders would leave us alone to make our own pace, we wouldn't have a problem.*" said Leaksville's Mayor.

"But, sir we have reports that verify that those measures you call progress are in fact being met with intense violence and sadistic opposition."

"*First of all, I would like to say to the people watching on television that our citizens are planning to uphold the Constitution of our great nation. We will work together to resolve this situation in a reasonable time and manner.*" added the Governor.

Then, there was a cut-away to a field reporter's film.

"We have investigated reports of harassment by the White citizenry of this town. Earlier today we were in front of a house, in this small town, where a White family has been the butt of evil acts: bricks through the windows of their home, their mailbox blown up (which is a Federal offense), dead animals left on their doorstep, threatening phone calls; the list goes on... Why? Because these White people had the audacity to invite and host their Black friends in their own home, and their fine upstanding White neighbors did not like it. Are we to believe that the right to choose our friends isn't one of the self-evident truths - an unalienable Right which our country was founded upon?" the reporter asked the television viewers all over the nation.

"Let's see what the neighbors of this family believe." he continued.

"I see someone looking out their window. Hello. Can I speak with you?

Oh, she pulled the shade down... Well, here's another person standing on the porch."

The reporter was running up and down the street.

"Good morning, we are doing a news report. May I ask you a question? Oh, he just slammed the door - guess he didn't want to talk with us... Here comes a car, maybe we can get them to stop... HELLO! Hello! hello! hello!"

Ed, Suellen, and their children sat absorbed in front of their 12" RCA.

"That's the same car that was driving up and down the street when we had our friends over." Ed remarked.

"Wow, he's not driving so slow now." Suellen replied.

The scene shifted as the same reporter continued his filmed account.

"Oh-my-goodness, they're at the Spring Church... Must-a-been some kind of meeting. There's Pastor Johns, all of da old folks, Professor Wright, Mr. 'n Mrs. Keys, de Shaw family, Iris 'n Natan Ross, Freesia 'n her children." Ed said. He was surprised; he was learning about things, through the news report, that had happened without his knowledge.

"I see J. K. Sage, 'n Sylvester 'n Begonia Willow; they're sitting with Deacon Riley 'n Delphine 'n the children are even wit' them... All da little children on Price Road seem ta be there… That's Nardu and some of the people from Black Bottom." Ed said as he watched the television in awe.

"We are here on Price Road at a meeting called by the leaders of the Black community… We are speaking with Professor Bill O. Wright, and Mr. and Mrs. Keys. Good afternoon. The church is full of people of all ages. There is a presence in this place of worship, it is an energy and excitement that is hard to describe. Would you tell the world what it is you hope to accomplish through this meeting?"

*"We want the White people to understand and recognize our steadfast position concerning our civil rights. We have been tolerant; we have been patient, we have been subservient for too many years. Our people are tired, we have waited long enough… Now is the time. Now Is The Time! NOW IS THE TIME!!**THE TIME IS NOW!!!***

The church building seemed to vibrate as the chant rose throughout the crowd.

The old folks said… *If you don't stand up for something, you will sit for anything.*

The old folks said… *Trouble strengthens your muscles, makes you stronger.*

The church ladies said… *How you endure the storm of life determines your destiny.*

Both the old folks and the church ladies said… *Never be mis-lead by the illusion of inclusion.*

1977

Suellen tightened her bra strap to counteract the effect of gravity on her once perky breast. Ed adjusted his glasses, and ran his fingers through his thinning white hair. They were driving down Price Road on the second Sunday in June 1977; it was a trip they had made every June for the past twenty years. They were headed to the Spring Baptist Church for a Homecoming/ Juneteenth celebration. The second Sunday in June was the date designated to acknowledge when the slaves in Texas found out they were free – two years after the fact. It was a date that Ed and Suellen O'Reilly marked on their calendar every year.

This year was particularly special because little Briar, who was not so little anymore, was being installed as the new pastor of Spring Church. Mr. Udell and his son, Tryee Udell, were going to be there with the buttons popping off their shirts, announcing: "That's my grandson! That's my nephew!" And, Ed planned to say, with a fake look of surprise in his eye, "Is that right?" Just the thought of creating that look on his face made the corners of Ed's mouth curl upward.

"Honey, is Freesia coming this year?" Ed asked his wife. Suellen maintained contact with Freesia Holley who moved to Columbus, Ohio many years ago to be with her children. Her oldest son settled there, after serving in Vietnam, and persuaded Freesia and his brother to come live with him. He told Freesia that it was time for him to take care of her since she had worked so hard all her life to take care of her family.

"Yeah, she's probably there already, they all were driving in on Saturday. They're bringing the new grandbaby with them." Suellen told him.

"Did you tell her our children won't be coming this year?" asked Ed, who had taken a two week vacation from his job as the Post Master General for the state of North Carolina. Neither of the O'Reilly children lived in the beautiful home Ed built for his family five years ago. Their oldest child was building homes and digging water wells in Africa with the Peace Corps; the youngest was working in Washington, D.C. as a researcher for a child advocacy organization.

"I almost wish someone would tear that chimney down; I still get a bad taste in my mouth every time I see it." Ed remarked as he drove past the old Ashford place. "Uncle DaDa and Mr. Sycamore said they were coming this year too. They haven't missed one of these homecomings since Ornella died."

Mr. Sycamore decided to move to Canada, with his nephew, about five years after Uncle DaDa went there. Ornella, Uncle DaDa's wife, did not adjust to the cold weather in Canada, and the lost she felt because of the fire never left her soul.

"Ornella caught pneumonia 'n she didn't seem the have the fortitude to fight." Mr. Sycamore said when Ed and Suellen tried to express to him their sympathy. "Death sent its mighty angel to take her to the land where there is only joy and no return." he remarked.

Mr. Sycamore and Uncle DaDa had spent several years registering mis-classified Indians from their Canadian home office. It had finally been disclosed that because of the Jim Crow and other racist laws many Indians had birth certificates and other documents that did not verify their true Indian heritage. Many were classified as white, others black, and still others mulatto – in some cases they all were within the same family. Because of the Indian's inability to read the English language, the mistake went unnoticed for many years.

During a conversation with Mr. Sycamore and Uncle DaDa, about their work of passion, Ed was stung by the research-your-family-tree-bug. It inspired him to talk to his family, in more depth, about their first hand family memories. In that investigative mode Ed discovered that one of his ancestors lived at Fort Christanna, VA during 1718 until it closed in 1720. Ed had heard Uncle DaDa's stories about the Fort. Ed knew something his relatives didn't know. He knew the people who were forced to stay at Fort Christanna were Indians – not soldiers. Ed knew that when the Fort was closed the United States Government herded the Indians on the Trail Of Tears, and stored them on reservations. Ed also knew that many Indians were left behind without the White man's knowledge.

The idea was to keep the Indian and Negro populations from getting together and birthing a prototype of an exceptional human being with talents a cut above any White man. The Indian's physical strength and intelligence, combined with the Negro's strength and strong cunning instincts, was a possibility that frightened the White population to the extent that they made every effort to keep the races separate. It didn't work… The White folks themselves created documents that added to their own deception because they could not look directly at a true full blooded Indian and be sure of what they were seeing. Ed found that the Cherokee Indians intermarried with the White population most often, those who knew did not speak of it.

Therefore, Ed was not shocked when his family research uncovered a Cherokee Indian great, great, great grandmother on his father's side His old analytical thought, of whether knowing about the truth of their ancestry would make a person different, came back over the years and tip-toed onto the surface of Ed's consciousness. He wondered what other secrets were in his family tree, and he felt a special connection to Mr. Sycamore and Uncle DaDa since he became aware of the Indian blood in his own family. When Ed looked in a mirror – he didn't look any different – didn't feel any different, but maybe that was because all his life he always tried to be true to his self. Uncle DaDa told Ed that genealogy investigations confirmed that there was hardly a Black family in America that did not have some Indian blood in their ancestry, and White people should not be surprised to find Indian blood in their genes. Indians did not die out quietly; instead, they procreated and multiplied.

Ed drove pass Illanna and Perry Wheatley's home place. They both were gone and their abandoned home long since decayed; their grave sites were in the back corner of the land belonging to their daughter, Iris, and son-in-law, Natan Ross. Ed glanced in the direction of the Wheatley home - toward where he knew the graves to be. At that moment, he had a spiritual awareness - the sense of seeing Illanna holding Perry's hand floating over their graves as they smiled at each other. It wasn't a vision that frightened him; in fact, Ed experienced a cozy warm sensation. Then, Ed noticed Miss Hag by the edge of the woods surrounding the cemetery; she was sitting as she always had - tall and erect on her horse with the fancy ties still on its tail. Without taking his eyes completely off Miss Hag, and still keeping his focus on the highway, Ed whispered to Suellen.

"Look straight ahead as the crows fly – that's the Miss Hag I told you about years ago. I didn't think she would still be alive. Wonder what she's doing here?" Suellen looked in the direction indicated, and replied at once in a soft voice that hardly escaped from the side of her mouth, "She is a strange looking one isn't she."

Ed remembered seeing Miss Hag at other times in the past twenty the years, but he had never been close to her; it was always a sighting from a distance, and she was always on the horse. He wondered if it could be possible that it was the same horse. How long did horses live anyway? And, how old was Miss Hag?

Ed remembered seeing Miss Hag the day of the Mc Donald accident. The Leaksville newspaper's front page story the next day was about the accident that left Mr. McDonald a virtual invalid, confined to a wheelchair. It was a strange occurrence. Mr. McDonald was collecting rent from Oliver Shaw; it was the seventh year of Jarrah's birth, and the third anniversary of Illanna and Perry's death. Oliver Shaw was feeding his pigs at the pig-pen across a field that once held string beans. The land was seasonally altered. Instead of walking the path around the flattened field, Dick McDonald took a shortcut across the middle of the bean field. Because he was looking straight ahead at Oliver Shaw, Dick McDonald did not look down at the ground where he was walking. He stepped on the tail of the rattlesnake that was laid, stretched out straight, sunning itself in the bean row. The huge snake leaped straight up and bit him on his groin, through his fancy suit; right on what he laughingly told his young wife, Elizabeth, on their wedding night were the family jewels. He screamed!!! Oliver Shaw turned to see Dick McDonald fall; he ran to get close enough to see what happened. Oliver threw the hoe that he carried down on the snake, and ran screaming for help. He told the reporters the story.

"That snake was so big I just threw the hoe and hoped it hit its mark. I wasn't about to stay around to see for sure, that was the biggest rattler I've seen, but I managed ta cut it in half. When I came back with help and more weapons, we had ta keep separating de halves; that snake kept trying to get its parts close. I hear-tell if de parts get close enough 'fore nightfall it could rejoin itself and live again! Well, nobody wanted that!" Oliver said

Mr. McDonald was rushed to the hospital; he was holding his manhood in both hands and screaming for dear life. It was such an ear-piercing noise that everybody on Price Road heard him; no matter where they lived, the noise reached their ears. Ed saw the activity when he just happened to drive pass the hospital when the ambulance was coming into the emergency entrance. That was when he saw Miss Hag riding bareback on her horse with the decorated tail. The horse seemed to glide, instead of trot, as it followed the ambulance down the street. Ed was stunned at the strange sight; he parked his car so he could watch the activity from an obscure spot. Ed observed Miss Hag as she sat erect and motionless on her horse while the medics rushed the wailing Dick McDonald, on a stretcher, through the automatic hospital doors as pedestrians walked by - ignoring the captivating sight that for him defeated analysis.

Mrs. McDonald rushed to her husband's side. The next morning the newspaper announced in bold print: **Mc DONALD NEUTERED BY SLEEPING SNAKE**

Ed remembered seeing Miss Hag at least one other time. It was the year after his job promotion; the year after his last day as the mailman on Price Road. The four young vigilantes, who set fire to Uncle DaDa's home, had spent the day in an old deserted barn. The atmosphere, in the barn, reeked of the ambiguities of purpose. The four friends had only accomplished one thing that day – to drink and smoke themselves into a drunken stupor. They always experimented in whatever way they could find to get high; the drug of choice that time was a concoction of: marijuana, beer, and a half a dozen aspirins diluted in each round of whisky. The result: the deep sleep that was associated with a drunken stupor and hot ashes from the lit cigarettes that dangled from uncoordinated fingers, then – **Fire!**

The flames could be seen for miles as the dry wood and residue of hay fed the inferno. Six moths later when they were able to talk about the fire, the men, all of whom had third degree burns over their bodies, told the same remarkable story.

"It twaz a weird feeling, I waz fully awake, I knowed wer I waz; I cudn't move, ma body just cudn't move!"

"It twas lik'I waz on da outside o' ma body, lookn'g in, an I couldn't get inta my body ta move it away from da fire. I saw da fire, but I cudn't feel it."

"I thought I heerd the hoof beat of'a horse trot, but twaz prob'bly just ma heartbeat. I'as scared…"

"Felt ma-self piss'n ma pants; I felt da pee run down'on ma leg, leav'ng a trail like what explode out o'a volcano. Da wetness was so hot; my body was melting!"

"I cou'd feel my skin swiv'ling of'a me; I waz becoming white *flesh!*"

"Felt like I wa in Hell… It waz weird!" was each man's remembrance. When asked, "How do you feel now?" each screamed out… "It hurt' now, I still feel it now! I hurt al'over!"

All of the townspeople flocked to the site of the burning barn; it seemed as if the world was being cremated - leaving a pungent smell. Ed got a glimpse of Miss Hag, sitting on her fancy tailed horse, watching the barn fire from a distance. It was only a fleeting glance, but Ed was almost sure it was Miss Hag. That fire was a tragedy that affected so many families in the White community. Four of their favorite sons almost lost their lives…

Ed thought about the grief his Pastor experienced when his grandson, who was one of those injured in the fire, had to spend the next years in rehab in the Danville Burn Center. The Pastor was the same man who led the church counsel meeting concerning Ed and Suellen's budding friendship with Colored folks. It was the same Pastor who told the TV reporters, *"God did not mean for the different races to cohabituate; he made us different, and he wants us to stay separated. You'll see… When you get to Heaven there will be a section for Whites, a section for Blacks; another section for the Brown and another for Yellow… But we can all get to our Heaven…"*

Ed and his family never stopped going to their church; they did not beat a retreat, even though they disagreed with the philosophy of its leader. It was their thinking that if change was to come within the church, the people of more progressive thinking needed to be there to witness and be a part of the miracle.

After the fire, Ed noticed a difference in the Sunday sermons. The Pastor seemed to have a more concerned and compassionate approach in his message; in fact, the Pastor changed his mind about Ed and Suellen's association with their friends from Price Road, and he made a special trip to their home to apologize for his role in their ostracism. Watching the process of change was reassuring to Ed. At least the Pastor was aware of the problem. And, after the fire that almost killed his grandson, the Pastor tried to help others in his congregation dig through the detritus of all the years of racial mis-teachings and mis-learning - to undo his part in the teaching of bigotry.

Suellen caused Ed's attention to shift to two 'beautiful' new houses with swimming pools in the backyards and brick columns that contained the mailboxes at the end of each driveway.

"Those must be the houses Sylvester and Begonia Willow and Lyndell and Zara Frasier built." Suellen said. "Zara promised to bring her toffee cookies; I hope she didn't forget." Suellen had made watermelon rind pickle and potato salad for the pot luck meal. She mimeographed copies of the recipes for anyone who wanted them; the recipe exchange had become a Homecoming tradition.

As they joined the cars parked beside the Spring Church, Suellen looked around at the crowd filing into the church. There was a time when the O'Reilly's were the only White people at Homecoming. Suellen realized that was no longer true, every year more and more people of diverse ethnicities were in attendance. More people from the North were retiring to North Carolina and Virginia, rather than Florida, because of the more consistent weather. They, for the most part, brought their lack of the slave holder's mentality and acceptance of the 1964 Civil Rights Act.; therefore, more and more open friendships between the races were visible. Dyed in the wool old Southern Whites had difficulty changing their thinking, but their children and grandchildren were watching television; they were more open to change. Friendships that garnered realms of opposition in 1957 were commonplace in 1977.

"I was right about the television wasn't I?" Ed said as he sought conformation of his prediction in the late 1950s. Suellen just slowly nodded her head in an affirmation that she understood.

In 1960 they watched the sit-in demonstrations in Greensboro, NC on television.

In 1961 the television showed the world James Meredith at the University of Mississippi escorted by Federal Troops for his protection.

In 1963 the entire world saw unbelievable scenes televised of Mr. Eugene "Bull" Connor with his fire hoses and police dogs.

The televised reports of the murder of Medger Evers on June 12, 1963 inspired many White people who had been silent, or undecided in the past, to stand up and be counted on the right side of the fence. They saw things that they couldn't imagine in front of their own eyes - on television.

On August 28th of 1963, Ed and all his family drove to Washington, D.C. with four busloads of people organized by the combined congregations of the black churches. The buses were overflowing; therefore, Ed and a few others drove their own cars following the buses. They sang, "We shall overcome...We shall overcome someday." It was a joy caravan traveling on the highway to the capital of the United States. When Martin Luther King told the President and Congress that he had a dream, Ed and his entire family were standing in the crowd to hear him. It was televised...

Suellen was watching the motorcade on television when President Kennedy was assassinated, and then the assassination of his murderer. Television captured the inauguration of Vice President Johnson into office as the 36th United States President. Americans saw President Johnson sign the Civil Rights Act, the law that made discrimination illegal, and gave the Federal Government power to enforce the law.

The mob atmosphere, rampant in the South, when three civil rights workers were killed in Philadelphia, Mississippi was televised all over the world. Television reported when the Supreme Court ruled that states could no longer ban interracial marriage.

Many White southerners such as Mr. Wallace, Gorge's father, who loved country music, found out from a televised concert that that one of their favorite Country Western singers, Charlie Pride, was a Colored man.

Sammy Davis Junior proved he was more than just a song and dance entertainer when he held his own in a televised debate with the snobbish intellectual William F. Buckley Junior.

Elvis Presley divulged, during a televised interview, that he developed his song and dance style because he loved to watch Colored entertainers and tried to imitate them.

Television showed the legal battle when the Georgia Legislature refused to seat Julian Bond in the State Senate after he won the election; it took a court battle before Bond was finally seated.

Thurgood Marshall was interviewed on television when he became the first African American Supreme Court Justice.

Dr. Martin Luther King was assassinated, and eye witness accounts were televised immediately.

The television cameras were there when Robert F. Kennedy finished a campaign speech just before he was assassinated.

Hank Aaron hit his 715th home run.

James Brown sang *I'm Black and I'm Proud* on television, and the world settled the question of what to call the descendants of Slaves.

Ed and Suellen entered the church quietly, and sat toward the back, nodding a sign of acknowledgement to those who looked their way. They glanced over the congregation… Ed was intrigued with the visual aspect of such a display of the natural color spectrum. The Homecoming celebration had become something akin to a beautiful horticulture garden; it was an integrated congregation, representative of so many races – so many colors, and everyone was welcomed.

"Is that J.K. I see in the choir?" Ed whispered to Suellen. Sometimes things looked fuzzy at a distance, Suellen told him he needed to get his eyes checked. Maybe he should because he was not sure that he really saw a fleeting intimate glance between the eyes of J.K. Sage and Delphine Green who sat on the opposite side of the choir stand. The tender look, he thought he saw, reminded Ed of Illanna and Perry; he smiled.

A rich baritone voice swelled to the rafters; at first, Ed didn't see the source.

"Amazing Grace"... The organ added layers of depth.

Then the Reverend, not so little anymore, Briar rose behind the carved walnut podium from the large ornate chair at the center of the dais; his voice and his arms stretched upward. Only his spit shined Florsheim shoes peeked out from underneath the long black robe; the flowing sleeves with velvet stripes gave the image of a large bird - perhaps an Eagle while the 6" bands of brightly colored imported cloth from Kenya rolled down both sides of the center front of the robe. The Reverend sang...

"Amazing Grace, Amazing Grace, How sweet the sound..."

He made one grand upward swoop with both arms, and the choir stood in unison in the back of the dais.

"If you know my past, you understand just how amazing my Grace is." The Reverend Briar said as he looked into familiar faces.

"That saved a wretch like me..." His baritone voice bellowed...

"Words written by a sinner; it could have been you or me. But this sinner was a slave trader who wrote those words when he came to realize that Jesus died for him too.

"I once was blind, but now I see."

"It is never too late to stop paying the wages of sin, to change your ways... to '**See**'." Reverend Blair said.

His presentation continued to be a combination of song and speech. It was not an emotional shouting of fire and brimstone, not a you-know-better lecture; Reverend Blair spoke as if he were having a thoughtful logical discussion; it almost seemed as if he were in a calm personal conversation with each member of the congregation.

Ed listened... *"I once was blind, but now I see..."* The Reverend, not so little anymore, Blair spoke and sang. Ed's insides churned with fresh enthusiasm as he sat in the pew holding onto Suellen's hand. A single thought emerged... Out there on Price Road, where God seemed to touch the earth with his favor, there was a continuing growth and development of human beings. Ed imagined his own personal conversation with God… "Are we being groomed for a test?"

Then, from somewhere deep inside Ed's core came the answer…

"YES," Ed imagined God to say. "And, the test is: Can your siblings, all God's children (my children) living in God's garden (my creation) - breathe the same air without strife?"

Ed squeezed Suellen's hand and looked around the sanctuary at all the worshipers; he looked out of the open stained glass window - down Price Road as cars with unknown people going to unknown designations drove past. It was another moment of epiphany for Ed; he felt as if he were a witness to a secret. He wondered if anyone could read the thoughts that went through his head… Was he the only one who knew? Ed thought…

*The people along Price Road are under observation… They Are Under Observation… THEY ARE All UNDER OBSERVATION… **WE ALL ARE UNDER OBSERVATION…***

Appendage

Professor Michele Bush uses Price Road as a class assignment:

Price Road
(Let's Talk About It)

Many things can be discussed in light of Price Road. First, we will look at the literary elements that permeate the text.

Plot

• *Characterization:* Ed is a major character. Rozlyn and Illanna can also be viewed as major characters. However, many minor characters have important roles.

• *Symbolism:* The names of the characters hold great symbolism. Aloe Vera is a great name for the health enthusiast who purports that natural remedies offer the best cures for what ails us. Most of the names of the Price Road residents are derived from the scientific names of plants, trees, or things that grow from God's earth.

- Metaphor

- Genre

• *Irony/ ambiguity:* The church groups provide the best irony. As Christians, we see them being less than Christian in their views of others and in their actions, most particular is their treatment of parishioners they deem as lesser than.

• *Theme:* War, education, and employment opportunities for Blacks vs. Whites, the church, male/female relationships.

There are other elements that can be explored as well.

Historical Context

• *Social, political, economic contexts:* These areas beg to be addressed. Rozlyn Berry is a great example of Blacks who tire of their treatment in rural Southern towns and decide to leave in pursuit of education and a better way of life. This is also seen in Ernest J. Gaines' "A Lesson Before Dying." Rozlyn's college education served her well. She wrote her family regularly, but Rozlyn did not return home to live. The current socio-economic conditions found in Northern cities such as Cleveland, OH; Philadelphia, PA; New York, NY; Chicago, IL is a testament to this occurrence. Ironically, many Blacks who fled the South during the Great Migration soon discovered that racism and ill treatment of Blacks were not confined to the South.

• *Ideology:* This can be tricky since one can view the treatment and return of Blacks who served in the military. Nardu is a great example. The lost of his limb occurred not due to battle but because there was no antiseptic available to treat a minor injury.
Claude McKay's poem, *"If We Must Die,"* is an excellent backdrop to Price Road because it addresses the issues of treatment of Colored soldiers during and after WWI.

• *Multiple voices:* The White community and their views and treatment of Blacks. Clyde Parker is an excellent candidate to explore. Despite the fact that it is apparent that well-to-do Whites look down on the poor White community, Clyde Parker sees himself as better than them although he is as poor as many of the Blacks along Price Road. Is there evidence of such today?

Readers of Price Road have suggested the book inspired the following starting points toward dialogue for one-on-one, small group, and book club conversations.

1. How does the author use the presence of snakes throughout Price Road?
2. Where and how does Miss Hag fit into society? How do the ideas of politically incorrect and apparent retribution relate with Miss Hags presence.
3. Why do we retain symbols from the past? What are those symbols along Price Road?
4. Can music provide nutrition for the soul, as food provides nutrition for the body? How important are music and food on Price Road?
5. What is the value of positive non-financial contributions to society? Does it make a difference? Which Price Road characters made such non-financial contributions?
6. In today's world could Begonia and Zara achieve the level of financial success they could in the 40's and 50's? Why?
7. A wise person once said, "Always be prepared." What does that mean? Is there anything people can do in today's world to always be prepared? How do some of the Price Road characters prepare themselves and for what?
8. What is the difference in Ed O'Reilly and Dick McDonald's view of women, race, and entitlement? Explore where people with those views may exist and how their views may become apparent.

Zara's Toffee Cookies

1 cup softened butter	2 cups flour
1 cup sugar	1 tsp. cinnamon
1 egg, separated	1cup chapped pecans or walnuts

1. Cream butter and sugar together until smooth.
2. Add egg yolk and mix in thoroughly
3. Sift flour, measure and sift again with cinnamon
4. Add flour to butter mixture – use hands to blend thoroughly
5. Spread mixture evenly over a greased cookie sheet [10" x 15"]
6. Beat egg white slightly – spread over surface of dough
7. Bake at 275° for 1 hour
8. Cut onto 1 ½ inch squares while hot
9. Cool

Suellen's Watermelon Rind Pickle

Rind from large watermelon	2 qts. cider vinegar
6 cinnamon sticks	1 cup lime powder
½ box pickling spice	½ cup salt
5 lbs sugar	

1. Peel all red meat and green skin from watermelon rind
2. Cut rind in 1" x 2" wide strips
3. Add 1 gallon cold water to lime
4. Add rind to lime water - soak overnight
5. Rinse thoroughly in fresh clean water
6. Cover with salted water and cook for 45 minutes
7. Rinse again
8. Boil in clear water for 20 minutes
9. Rinse well again
10. Combine sugar and vinegar in a large non-reactive pot – heat to dissolve sugar

11. Place spices in a cheesecloth pouch and suspend with kitchen twine into the pot
12. Add rind to the pot
13. Bring to boil – reduce heat and simmer for 2 hours
14. Let sit overnight
15. Store in canning jars